TENEŌ

A novella

Kojo Gyan

Teneō

latin. verb.

- To hold, have.
- To possess, occupy.
- To watch over, guard, defend.

I.

I live for the moments in-between.

Those precious seconds of flight.

Adrenaline.

Freedom.

If only it lasted longer—days or even hours. But the pain sets in immediately. I can already feel it needling at the boundary of my form. And now it's off to the next before I start to unravel.

Inhabiting a new host brings an end to the pain. And while I mourn the loss of my own form, the safety of this corporeal body is a relief—a worthwhile trade of freedom for security.

Alive behind the eyes of a human who is so lost in thought they won't notice me feeding on that slipping consciousness. And when that consciousness returns, I'll be evicted and forced to look for the next person.

And then the next.

And the next.

But in those moments in-between, I'm free.

I feel the others around me constantly, not with eyes, or ears or

any of the unsightly appendages humans have. I can't see them.
I'm just . . . aware of the conscious energy flitting around me,
materializing and then unraveling into nothing.

With how much you humans interact, that must seem strange.

When I inhabit a host, I'm amazed by how much time humans
spend paying attention to each other, no doubt due to all their
external senses.

Sounds.

Sights.

Smells.

It's all a bit too much. Too much noise, too much attention.
Where can you go that other humans can't sense you?

I don't want that.

I would like to occasionally know how others of my kind live.

How they feel.

Occasionally, when I'm inhabiting a host, I do see them, if only
for a moment. A tricky bit of light here. An odd shadow there.
I hear them sometimes as well. A whistle as they move past, a
painful howl as they unravel and blink out of existence.

Do you ever see us?

Would you know how to look?

Are we as foreign to you as you are to us?

II.

Another unravels to my right.

Its howl snaps my host out of his trance, and his consciousness nudges me out of his mind.

I'm flying again—formless and free.

My boundary starts to ripple, but it'll wait a little longer. It's morning, and there is no shortage of hosts in the city center.

I follow one along the sidewalk.

He's at the beginning of a block, meaning the next crosswalk is not for a while. There's plenty of time for the human's mind to wander and more time for me to safely share his consciousness.

The additional seconds of lazy flight are well worth the now-stabbing pain around me.

The moment I make contact with him, the pain flows away, and his world snaps into view.

Shorter than most.

I'm not seeing the tops of the other human's heads like last time. I also can't see into the endless windows and buildings.

Not that he's helping much.

His eyes are pointed low and close, permitting me only to see a short distance in front of him.

The audio experience isn't bad.

This human has something in his ear, and the sounds flowing in from it are rhythmic.

So far, I enjoy these types of humans the most. Human senses are so overwhelming, so having one or two that are limited makes it much easier for me to focus on the others. And I don't have to see the faces of other humans as they see, hear, smell, and feel me walk by.

Well, not me. My host.

The sidewalk is kind of pretty. It has a neat and rigid structure, just like the buildings that rise from it. To your eyes, they seem so strong. In my natural form, I would move through them as if they were nothing.

Pain!

I didn't see it. Something dripped onto my host's hand from the cylinder we were holding. Something hot. The pain snaps his consciousness back into place and pushes me out.

III.

That was the first time I've felt human pain.

Your pain is so localized . . . so pointed.

The pain I feel in my form is much more broad. It's everywhere.

Less intense . . . for now. But it radiates from my core out to my boundary and back. No need to worry about it now. Another host passes by so close that I can easily occupy her.

This one is uncomfortable. Every step lingers with pain as high arching heels make contact with the ground.

She's a storm of senses.

Taller than the last host, her gaze is crowded with the uncountable humans, objects and buildings of the streets beyond. She's got nothing in her ears, and all manner of sounds assault her. And she's cold. Her arms, shoulders and legs are exposed to the wind.

How do you function like this?

From her vantage point, I can see that we've moved away from the densest part of the city. Crowds melt behind us as my host takes us through a series of side streets to a quieter area.

This will make things more difficult. The fewer people there are, the less viable hosts there will be, and the more danger I'm in.

If I can't find a host quickly, or if I lose the connection to this one
. . .

I don't want to think about it.

For the time being, at least, that doesn't seem to be a concern.

She passes through quieter city streets and comes upon an open expanse of grass and trees. What do you call them again?

A park.

My host's memories flow into me with an answer to my question—another benefit of sharing your consciousnesses.

They're better. These parks.

Better than the uniform sidewalks and strong buildings.

They feel like so much more. They're alive.

And the people within them look so much more at ease than the ones milling about inside the buildings.

I'm beginning to lose my grip on this host's consciousness. I can feel it as she approaches the small truck on the side of the park.

Searching the edges of her periphery, I see a handful of people around. One of them, perhaps? The woman taking the steaming cup from the man in the truck is positively bouncing with energy. The couple to the right of my host is caught in a lively conversation. The young man who runs past is yelling at a small creature.

All of them are too present to be a viable host.

One of them has a smaller animal.

A dog.

If only I could inhabit the lower life form's mind, but none of them seem to have the capacity, probably because their consciousness isn't as complex as a human's.

My host reaches the truck, and I'm thrown out of her.

I don't have the security to enjoy my flight this time. I need to find a new host quickly.

Needles prickle the edge of my boundary. How much time do I have?

I race back to the busy side of town, keeping my awareness open in case a viable host passes.

I can feel the humans around me, but none of them leak any conscious energy.

Stabbing pains shoot from my boundary to my core.

I need to find someone.

This hasn't happened for such a long time, not since my infancy. I've learned too much in the last few days to be this careless! I should have checked the last woman's direction before inhabiting her.

Wait!

At the far end of the park, I see a steady stream of conscious energy. No time to waste.

I leap.

IV.

The pain subsides, and my host lets out a breath of relief.

No.

I did that.

I breathed.

Sighed. My host corrects—the voice of her memories explaining the concept.

Her voice surprises me. It shouldn't. Every host I've ever inhabited has one, but there's something different . . .

It feels like no one else is here.

Usually, when occupying a body, I can feel the human's link to their consciousness as they wander. Some part of them is always tethered to the body: controlling movements, breathing, and processing in the background.

But right now. It's just me.

This body isn't moving. Or, it wasn't until I sighed, at least.

I have all the same senses. I can hear the cars and people in the distance, smell the foul stench of garbage from the nearby dumpster, feel the wind pick up and toy with my host's hair, and taste the minty gob in her mouth. I can even see.

I see everything.

I moved her eyes. Her eyes can move.

Not only that but so can her head and her body. I'm in full control. I can turn her around. I can look up and down the street, beyond the colorful garments on my sleeves, to the variety of row houses and smaller buildings rising from the sidewalk. The inside of my chest starts beating. I've experienced humans exerting themselves physically once before. Why is it happening now?

"Are you okay, Miss?"

Another human. Younger. He's staring at me.

I wonder . . .

"Yes," I hear my host say before I can try to speak.

And just like that, I'm out. Flying in my natural, formless state.

How?

I didn't even feel her consciousness return. To go from nothing to everything like that is unlike anything I've felt. How did it happen? Even before that, why was there no trace of her until that moment?

I stay close, fluttering around her, unable to see, hear or smell. What I wouldn't give for her senses now. I want to understand what happened.

I don't have much time, though. Soon, the pain will . . .

The pain will . . .

The pain . . .

. . . there is none.

$\mathcal{V}.$

I feel . . . full.

Satiated.

I've never felt this before, nor considered whether it was possible.

The urge, the hunger, the thing that pushes me to move from person to person and spend as little time in between as possible. I had never considered it could be stopped, that it was responding to a need that could be met.

But now . . .

It must be connected.

That emptiness. The control over that last host. My current state. They must be connected.

Can I do it again? Do I even want to?

The only reason I inhabit humans is to stop the pain. To prolong my life. I imagine it's the same for others like me.

Isn't it?

If the pain is gone, is there a point in inhabiting a new host? To leave the in-between? What else would I do?

Is it really gone?

I'm feeling something on my boundary. Not pain. Not quite.

A sort of . . . numbness. It's a little different from before. But is it the prelude to pain restarting?

Maybe I didn't eliminate it . . . I just staved it off for a while.

I should be cautious.

In my excitement, I've let myself drift upwards, away from the ground and the crowds of consciousness, towards the sky and the warmth of the sun.

I've never thought it was possible to fly that high before. But I've always wanted to.

Sometimes, I feel vague consciousnesses far above me, but they're so out of reach that I'd likely dissolve out of existence before I reach them. I wonder what they are. More humans who have found their way into the sky? Or some other type of conscious energy like me and my kind.

Or maybe something else entirely.

A tingle runs from my core to my boundary. It itches.

It's uncomfortable.

The pain will come back soon. I'm sure of that now.

I veer back to a more concentrated part of the city, swarms of consciousness going every which way. Some are below, moving fast, and some are crammed into the buildings rising out of the sidewalk.

There are plenty of available hosts.

Are there more of you like the last host? Different ones. Special ones.

The way that felt. To not be in pain. To fly freely . . . and be in complete control of a human body.

I need to find another like the last—one whose consciousness has completely lapsed. One who will make it possible for me to stay in-between longer. One who will be more fun to inhabit in the meantime.

I should have followed the girl instead of losing myself in the moment. Maybe she's different?

But I didn't notice anything before I took control of her, and looking at the swarms of humans before me, I don't notice anything now.

Needles.

The pain has started again.

Time to choose one.

I will try one that is crammed into one of these buildings. The pain subsides as I merge through the wall and into his consciousness.

And the world, as defined by human senses, explodes before me.

I can hear the din of too many other humans, but I can't see them.

I can't see much, in fact. My vision keeps dipping in and out as his head falls and raises and his eyes close and open.

I'm sitting in a rather comfortable chair and leaning on a small desk in what appears to be a small compartment. In front of me is a screen with numbers, letters and images.

I'm not moving, but specifically, I don't have the ability to move this host. This one is ordinary.

Maybe it really is just the girl who was exceptional . . .

Or maybe I just need to try more hosts.

I leap. For the first time, I'm leaving the safety of a host by choice. It's exhilarating and painful.

I wasn't in the host long enough to stave off much of the pain. The needles still tear at my boundary.

There has to be another one like her.

This time, it's a larger room where many humans sit around a large table, all looking at a screen together. I can't move this one either. I'm stuck staring at the table just in front of the speaker.

Another leap.

This one kicks me out nearly as soon as I land. I catch a brief glimpse of some sort of machine—a box with numbers and a window. It whirrs slightly as my host leans on the counter next to it. My host's consciousness snaps back as soon as the machine dings.

It doesn't matter. I'd had enough time to confirm he wasn't exceptional, either. I was sharing his consciousness. I didn't have control like with the other girl.

I will find another one.

$\mathcal{VI}.$

I need a break.

I'm wearing thin. My boundary has shrunk and I'm less now than I've ever been. The burning, slicing pain threatens to tear me apart. No matter the quality, I need to stay in this host a little longer.

Thankfully, that doesn't seem to be an issue.

This one trudges along the sidewalk. Uncomfortable, restrictive clothing clings to him, close to strangling from a piece of fabric around his neck. Heavy case in one hand.

It's not the most comfortable of occupations. But it's merely uncomfortable. Not painful.

The view is boring.

His gaze is focused straight down at the sidewalk. It's not high enough for me to see the humans around him using his peripheral vision.

I've started to get good at that.

Noticing other humans and telling them apart by their features. It's been useful.

I'm starting to realize that, through human eyes, there are queues for when another human becomes available to inhabit—a relaxing of their facial and body muscles. If I hadn't figured that out, I wouldn't have been able to go through as many hosts as I did today.

I've also started to notice something else.

I don't think humans can see conscious energy. Too often today, I've witnessed another of my kind's demise and heard the howls of their unraveling. But it never seems to disrupt the host I'm in.

They also don't seem to be able to tell when another of their own kind's consciousness slips.

So many times, I've inhabited someone as they are in an interaction with another, suddenly assaulted by lengthy speeches detailing someone's life, opinions and petty gripes.

It's very confusing that the host stopped listening halfway and that the other continued speaking after.

Is this common for you humans?

In any case, these realizations have made me focus more on the conscious energy I see. If this is something unique to my kind, there must be some clue to help me differentiate between exceptional and non-exceptional hosts, right? That is . . . if there are any other exceptional hosts.

I keep worrying that perhaps that girl from yesterday was the only one.

My host moves slightly left to avoid a passerby.

A drunk. His inner voice volunteers.

It's a difficult concept to understand. But if I understand correctly, this is a different conscious state humans can be in, and that may be worth testing.

If only I could turn this head to get a better look.

I'll have to risk it.

I leap from my host.

Pain radiates through me. That wasn't a long enough respite, but I can see the drunk now. His consciousness is leaking.

It's not normal. There's so much of it.

This is it!

I finally found another. He's vacant, just like the girl.

VII.

I've found another exception.

There are differences. But they may just be the difference from host to host.

This one smells.

It's a powerful assault on the nose that undoubtedly comes from the dirtier clothes he wears. There's also a taste in his mouth that I don't much care for. But stranger still are his movements.

I'm able to move and walk. I can turn my head. But everything is slightly askew.

My host's movements go almost in the direction I desire, but my balance seems off. I lurch to the side and almost collide with another human walking the other way.

"Watch where you're going, you drunk!" he yells.

That word again. There's something I don't understand. What is drunkenness?

The host's inner voice tries to help, but the answer is unintelligible.

Strange.

My vision is worse. I can barely recognize the features of passing humans. Everything is behind a blurred veneer.

Still . . . this is what I was looking for.

I wonder how long I'll have control of this one and how I should use the time I do have.

The door of a building next to me opens and I enter.

The majority of the hosts I inhabit stir or wake when crossing thresholds. It's not something I've gotten to do often.

I'm in a completely different place. Gone is the sidewalk, and instead, smooth stone tiling lines the inside of a shopping mall.

"Hey! I thought I told you you're banned from here!" a large man in a blue and black uniform says.

He is known to my host but not to me.

Again my host's inner voice tries to explain, and again, the explanation is unintelligible.

"Are you listening to me?"

The man in black and blue looks even more intense. He is expecting an answer.

I've never spoken before. I want to try.

"Hello."

I did it!

"Hello? Jesus Christ, how drunk are you?"

Apparently, that wasn't the right response. He grabs my shoulder and leads me out of the mall.

"I'd like to stay inside," I say.

"I bet you would," he replies. "Come back when you're sober."

I don't understand. Sober? Who or what is that? Why is it a requirement to enter a building?

Another unintelligible reply comes from my host's inner voice. But I do manage to understand that sober is the opposite of drunk.

No matter. I'll go elsewhere.

Ow.

What is that? *Pain.* From the host, but it's . . . inside?

It's near me.

In the host's head. I feel it as waves crashing against the sides of his head. I hadn't noticed it before, but it's starting to intensify. His vision is also worsening. And there's something coming up from his stomach.

"Oh my God!" a passing woman screams as I let out whatever was coming up. "That's so gross."

More is coming. I can feel it.

"You gotta go, buddy! Get out of here!"

The man in black and blue is back, pushing me further down the sidewalk, but I can barely pay attention to him. My host's vision is spinning, the waves crashing in my head have gotten louder, and I can feel more coming up.

This is too unpleasant.

I leap!

It's a strange feeling going from the discomfort and pain of this human into the painless relief of my natural form.

I've expanded—free again in the moments in between.

And now I know that the woman was not the only one of her type that exists. My experience with her was more pleasant than this one, but there are others out there.

I just need to find them.

VIII.

Complete control.

My host's feet are stable underneath me. His movements are sharp and reflexive.

I can move all his appendages independently. I can look where I want: from the sidewalk below me to the sky above to the seemingly endless rows of small residential buildings in this part of the city.

This is my fourth one.

First, the drunk, then an older woman in the mall, then a young boy in a school, and finally, this young man who has simply been roaming the streets.

His hand runs the length of the building beside me as I walk. Proportionally small hands feeling the crags of the stone exterior as I go. This one isn't so bad.

I may have liked the older woman more. While her movements were stiffer and more uncomfortable if done quickly, she was tall and graceful. Her vision was poor, however, so I returned her to the store she was working at after a brief tour around the mall.

The young boy's body wasn't the problem, although it was a little short. His movements were lithe, his vision was perfect, his energy boundless. But his incarceration in school was more than I could bear. It had taken me several attempts to leave the class-room, and even when I succeeded, I still wasn't able to leave the school. I grew tired and left him talking to the principal.

And now this one.

I'm somewhat limited by his proportions: an awkward amalgam of short legs, a long torso, small hands, and large feet. But free, at least in his ability to traverse the city.

I wonder how the girl is doing. That first one with the long hair and the minty taste.

I stop my host from moving across the crosswalk.

We're close.

I turn up the street.

These types of humans are so few and far between that I've exhausted practically all the conscious energy I've been able to absorb from them while trying to find the next one.

Ive travelled further around the city than I've ever been, across several city blocks into uncountable buildings—all the way up and down their floors.

It's . . . unsatisfying.

Despite my size, I'm still spending all the time in between searching for my next host. Despite my growth, I'm still at risk of unraveling. Despite my control, I've done nothing I haven't experienced in a human form.

My host's ungraceful steps carry me up one more street. I can see the entrance to a city park, and I start scanning the area.

I don't want to look for hosts anymore.

To scurry from one to the next just to stave off death.

With these exceptional human hosts, I should be able to sustain myself on one if I stay within it for a longer term.

As long as it's the right one.

A chill runs through me as my host steps onto a familiar park path. It's something I've felt in my natural form, like a wave of conscious energy intersecting me.

But how?

I'm enclosed. Within a host, my conscious energy shouldn't be exposed. Or at least that's what I—

That thought is cut short as my host's eyes lock on the figure exiting a building not far from where my path picks up.

A girl.

Small. Soft. Dark-haired.

Bright-colored clothing. A familiar grace to her movements.

Is it her?

I try to remember.

Colorful clothing, certainly. She had been short.

It could be her.

We're in the same park.

She approaches and I strain my eyes, looking for the telltale signs.

It has to be her.

I leave my current host without a thought. It's well worth the risk.

I feel for a plume of leaking conscious energy and find it immediately.

It's her.

She's the one.

IX.

My host's mouth splits open.

She's smiling.

We're smiling.

I can't help it. The giddiness I feel is ringing through our body. My feelings and my host's feelings are one.

Fascinating.

I can't waste time, though. I don't know how long I'll have this time, and I need to learn everything I can about her—anything that will help me identify her next time.

There's a small body of water nearby . . . a fountain. I need to take in every detail I can.

She's small. Not just her height but her build. Slight. Curly hair. Pointed face. There's something on her face . . . glasses. Round. Large. The hue of her skin is very middle-of-the-road, neither the darkest nor lightest I've seen.

I wish there were something that stood out more. How do you humans recognize each other when you all look so similar?

She's covered in colorful clothing, but that can change. So can the glasses, I suppose.

I need more.

Where was I leaving?

Home.

Her voice is clear and melodic despite its distance from the surface.

How do I get in there?

A key. It's in my bag.

This is perfect. Knowing where she lives will make it easier to find her later. And even if her consciousness returns on the way there, I'll be able to follow her.

"I've never seen you before."

Who?

A man. Awkwardly built with strange proportions.

My former host? But why? How?

"Why this one specifically?"

What?

"Do you not know how to speak yet?"

A crooked smile plays at his lips. Amused. His face is still slack, but there's something behind his eyes.

"I can speak," I force out. Her voice is soft. Higher than his.

I like it better.

He eyes me without saying anything. With an ungraceful yawn, he stretches his arms and looks over his body.

"This one's proportions are unusual," he says as if he just realized.

"You're like me," I realize.

"Yes," he answers. "Older, I would guess. Why her?"

"She . . ." I trail off, looking for an explanation. "She's different."

He nods and walks around me and my host.

"I get what you mean. I've been watching this one," he says. "She belongs to you?"

"Belongs?"

I don't understand.

He's amused again.

"I'm the first one you've ever interacted with? Of us, I mean."

I make my host nod. "Yes."

He starts walking towards the end of the park and waves for me to follow.

"You should come with me," he says. "I'll introduce you to more."

I want to.

But . . .

I look down at the keys in my hand. I can't afford to lose this host without seeing where she lives. And who knows how long I'll have control.

"I can't," I say.

He doesn't look surprised. Or disappointed.

"You don't know how much longer you have?"

He turns and grins. He knows something I don't.

"You must be very young," he says as he walks away. "I'll let you have that one for now since I can take this one as a consolation prize."

Consolation prize?

A thing given to one who doesn't win, my host defines.

I don't understand.

"Don't worry," he yells back as if hearing my thoughts. "I'll come and find you later after you've had some time to enjoy your body and learn some more."

𝒳.

Another one of my own kind.

I just spoke to another of my own kind.

Should I follow him? I want to learn more. He seemed to know how long I could stay in this host, but how could he? How did he even know I was inside this host?

No, I need to stay focused.

I don't know how long I have. No matter what he said, I need to figure out how to find her again.

Her home isn't far.

One step is enough to reinforce my decision to stay. She's perfect. Her stride is so unencumbered.

So graceful.

I'm tempted to go even faster.

Temptation wins and I burst forward on her toes.

She's so light.

And this feeling . . .

The wind rushes past in bursts, whipping her hair behind me.

Why don't you humans always move like this?

She's smiling again. And something else . . . breath falling out of her.

What is it? *Laughter.*

It's exhilarating.

Stop.

I'd almost missed the building—my host's home.

There are not many steps leading up to the doorway, but I'm having some trouble climbing them. My host's legs are weak, and I'm struggling to breathe in as much air as her body seems to need. There's also a thumping in the center of my host's chest.

What is this?

Tired.

Low on energy?

Interesting. You humans also have a limited supply of energy powering your forms. Until I learn how to replenish it I'll have to be more selective about when I choose to use the full capabilities of this body.

My host's hand coils around the rusted door handle. Solid. Un-moving. Human barriers are so annoying. So needlessly imper-meable.

I could simply pass through this door in my natural form, but I doubt she could manage it. There must be a way.

The lock.

Ah, I see it!

There's a small slot in the door above the handle. I can see a piece that fits that slot. It's in her bag.

My host seems to have a number of these keys, all attached to a ring. But I know the one I need—the two, actually. From what I see, I will need two keys: one to get inside and one to get inside my host's specific door inside the building.

The door swings open as I turn the key and handle.

It's hard not to marvel at what you humans have built. In my own form, even though I can pass through the barriers and the buildings, I find them tiresome—a kind of disruptive noise disturbing my freedom. But with the senses of a human, it's amazing how well you've curated the world to your senses.

The door shuts behind me, and the noise of the outside fades. The cool wind disappears, and the dull light of the fading sun is replaced by a bright lamp.

It's quiet. It's warm. It's safe.

The interior feels softer. Smoother. The walls are colorless where they aren't made of wood. The wood itself is shiny and smooth. And the floor, a lighter shade of wood, gives way just the slightest amount under my feet.

I start up the stairs, another human invention I appreciate. For all your lack of mobility up and downwards, you humans haven't let it stop you from reaching higher and lower areas.

I'll take the stairs slowly until I figure out how to replenish this body. I wonder how I do that?

Rest. Eat.

Rest? How? Do I just stop doing anything? Will that work? And eat what exactly? Does it matter?

No answer.

It must not matter as long as I accomplish both of those things.

We've reached the third floor and my host's door. I slide her key into the door, open it and step in.

Brightness is my first observation.

The door opens into a small hallway, but the walls are light, bright colors—pink and yellow. Some fading sunlight comes from beyond the hallway.

The light comes from a very large window covering the entire far wall.

My host's entire home appears to be this one room in addition to the hallway and the bathroom off to the side. It has a window on one wall and a kitchen on half of the other. On opposite ends of the room are a bed and a desk, with a sofa and a small TV in the middle.

I'm a little disappointed that there isn't anything in this room I haven't already been exposed to through other hosts.

I had thought this host was special. But perhaps what makes her special is only my connection with her.

But what about the other? He had also been watching her.

I don't know what to do now.

I've never been in a body for this long.

I'm beginning to miss my previous form. Standing in this small room, in this small building, trapped in this limited human body makes me want to fly. I want to be free.

But I shouldn't leave until I'm forced to. I've spent too much time searching for other hosts today, and if I do this right, I should be able to stay in my form far longer if I take advantage of every moment in this host.

I need to find something to do.

I wander over to the desk. There are a number of photos of my host pinned above it—some with other humans, some without.

In one picture my host holds onto some skin at her hip. The note above says only "fifteen lbs."

Weight loss. Her inner voice explains to me. Through pictures and images, I ascertain that she wants to be smaller but has made no progress.

A whole section of photos grabs my attention. Strange land-scapes. Impossible structures. People of different shapes, colors and sizes. A note above reads "Travel."

Her inner voice defines the section for me. She quietly shares her aspirational excitement about visiting different areas of the human world, for seeing far-off and difficult-to-explain things, for experiencing things she has never experienced.

I want to know more. What else has she seen? Where else has she been?

Silence. *Regret.*

It's hard to decipher feelings. But it is clear enough that my host hasn't been able to "travel" as much as she has wanted. Too many other obligations.

But that will change. That much is clear from her intent. She will travel.

Maybe I can travel with her?

My eyes search the rest of the pictures on the board. There's one of my host in this room . . . but the room looks better. Less strewn about and in a slightly different format.

I like it better.

I wonder if I can put it back using the picture as a guide.

XI.

I'm back.

I spent hours getting my host's house in order, looking through her belongings, spending as much time with her as she would allow, and then some time afterward watching her consciousness fall asleep.

Flying. Free. Formless.

There's no pain at my boundary. It's like before. I'm barely even aware of it.

No.

That's not true. It's just farther away.

I can feel my boundary move when I do, but it's distant. Silk swaying around my core.

I've expanded.

Maybe that's the wrong word. I'm still formless and my general size is irrelevant.

But I am more.

The night sky is clear and calm.

I'm flying directly into it . . . the same thing I did the first time I left this host—something that wasn't possible for me before.

It's so different in the sky than it is on the ground.

Quieter.

There is less human-conscious energy, although there are still some in tall buildings. And there's that occasional energy I can sense far above me. But nothing like the ground level, where humans are constantly crawling over each other.

There's also less . . . death.

On the ground, I can constantly hear the screams of my kind as they burn out from lack of sustaining energy. With greater size I can also feel more of my own kind intersect me as they try to outrun the ticking clock of their demise.

But not up here.

Up here, it's calm. It's quiet.

I want to go higher. And I think I can.

I'm larger than I've ever been. And there's not even the remotest sense of pain at my boundary.

I swim through the cooling air. Further upwards. Towards the stars. Away from the city lights.

A chill.

A wave of conscious energy. It's similar to what I feel when I'm intersected.

One of us.

My kind.

And it's not just one.

There are several up here.

Large. Unfathomably so.

I can feel them as our boundaries intersect. It's not communication, as you humans would put it, but awareness.

But it's more awareness than I've ever felt. I guess I've never been large enough for my boundary to intersect with another's to this degree.

How many of them are there?

And how did they grow to become this large?

Can you not speak yet, young one?

The voice reverberates within me. Passing into my boundary through the intersection. How?

It is too early for you. Go back down until you learn.

The words are kind. Truthful, without judgment or rebuke. I'm reminded of the other I met on the ground.

Go back down, young one. You are in danger. Mind your boundary.

My boundary?

I've shrunk. Not much, but definitely some. More than I should have by now.

How? No answer.

Go.

The voice is right. I am in danger, though I don't know how.

I start my descent.

XII.

For the second time, I've spoken to another of my own kind. And for the second time, they've commented on my age.

Young one.

I've missed something—potentially multiple somethings.

How did the ones above become so large? How could the one from yesterday tell my age at a glance?

What are they both expecting me to learn?

I need to find out.

I slow my descent, hovering in the air to survey the night sky.

What should I do next?

XIII.

Hours.

I've been free for hours.

No pain. No hosts. No threat of unraveling into nothing.

Flowing through the cool, dark expanse of the city.

So quiet.

Most humans aren't conscious (or even half-conscious); their minds are shut off as their bodies rest. It's almost unbelievably still.

Serene.

My thoughts drift to a particular picture from my newfound host's picture board: an empty expanse of sun, sky and sand. I wonder if this is what it's like.

I've strayed pretty far from her apartment by the park. Through the center of downtown, out the other side to an area I've never spent that much time in.

It's lower here.

Less barriers erected by humans. Emptiness to one side except for a number of small lower life forms beneath the surface.

There's also less of my kind out here. I hear their screams far less often as they burn out.

Nighttime is the worst for that.

The worst time for me, too.

Until tonight.

I like the dark, the emptiness. I want to fly a little further until I hear nothing.

Is that possible?

Not yet.

My boundary is too small to stray much further. It's not painful, but I'm more aware of it. I can feel the hem of my form tug as I fly through the night sky.

I'll need to feed soon.

But I should have enough time to make it back into the higher area of town. Through the denser clusters of humans. Into the park and up to that apartment building.

Back to where she sleeps.

XIV.

She's awake already.

Or perhaps it's more accurate to say she's not asleep.

Conscious energy leaks out of her like smoke, signaling her receptiveness to occupation.

I leap.

It feels familiar already, this small, soft human form. This small apartment. The easy control of a fitting form.

I wonder how it feels for her.

Awake when other humans ought not to be. Hours before the sun will rise. Awake but not conscious.

I'm in the smallest of the rooms in her apartment—the bathroom.

I'm holding something, but it's too dark to see what it is.

Where are the lights?

Wall. Switch, her inner voice whispers.

I flick the switch, and with the lights on, I can see my host in the mirror above the sink.

She's less clothed than when I was here last.

I like her form.

She's small. Soft. As graceful as a gangly human could possibly be.

I'm holding a bottle of small things.

Pills. Sleeping pills.

I drop them.

If my host were to sleep, her consciousness would be closed off from me, and I need to feed for a little longer.

I like being less clothed.

Feeling the warm air on her skin.

The cold floor of the bathroom, the kitchen and then the living room on her feet.

Why don't you humans spend more time this way?

With the lights on. I can see that my host has not ruined the work I did earlier to reorder her living space. There have been some changes, though.

I wander over to the picture board to re-inspect my host's hopeful travel pictures. There's something new on the small board with the picture of her clean room: a small Post-it note with a circle drawing and symbols.

Smiley face, her voice interprets and defines for me.

My host's lips creep open at the edges and warmth floods inside her body as I understand the meaning and the effect my actions had.

Happiness.

I look to see if there's anything else I can tidy up. A set of clothing has been placed nearby in a neat pile. And there is . . . something on the counter.

A dish?

Covered in thin plastic, with a note on top.

"Breakfast: 2.5 minutes on medium."

Oh, it's food! I've seen humans eating food before, but I've never tried.

What does that second part mean?

Microwave.

A wave of information. Too much all at once.

But I understand the basics of what I have to do.

The plastic falls away from the bowl with a tug. I don't like the feeling. It clings to my skin.

I toss it to the side and put the bowl in the box known as the microwave. After a couple of attempts, I set the time, and the microwave whirs to life.

I have to wait now.

May as well take a look at the other change my host made.

The set of clothing left out offends me. After all I did to ensure the clothing didn't ruin the aesthetic of this small room, she's made the same mistake as before.

But at least this one is set out neatly.

Another note.

"Clothing for tomorrow."

The whirring stops with a loud ding.

The microwave. It's done! Forget the clothing for now.

Hot. Despite being cool to the touch only moments ago, the bowl is much too hot to touch right out of the microwave.

Breath and smiles fall out of my host as I watch the steam come off of whatever is in the bowl. How amazing your human inventions are!

The fragrance coming from the bowl is intoxicating.

The voice of my host tells me the name of the scents I'm picking up.

Cinnamon. Brown sugar. Apples. Oatmeal.

Maybe I can get some out without touching the bowl.

I use the spoon to maneuver some of the oatmeal out of the bowl without removing it from the microwave.

I'm getting better at navigating human bodies.

The heat of the oatmeal hurts my mouth, but it doesn't matter. What a powerful sensation! Or sensations. There are so many all at once.

Sweet, spiced flavor.

Heat.

An altogether unpleasant lumpy texture.

I want another bite!

My host's voice shows me how to blow on the spoon to cool the oatmeal down.

It's more of the same but still just as powerful.

Without the pain from the heat, I notice some other sensations: the soft rigidity and tartness of the apple, which has a better texture and some creaminess.

Incredible.

Do you humans experience flavors like this all the time? I understand why I've never had this experience. Who would let their consciousness wander while experiencing sensations like this?

Even with the unappealing texture.

You humans have so many senses.

I'll have to keep track of the ones I like and the ones I don't for future reference.

So far, I like being less clothed, running and eating. I don't like being overly clothed, the texture of oatmeal, and interacting with other humans.

What else is there?

What else would my host do this morning?

Shower and get dressed.

The idea of putting on more clothes doesn't appeal to me. But the shower concept, if I understand correctly, seems to involve less clothing and an intense feeling of warmth.

I'll try that next.

But first.

I drop the finished bowl of oatmeal on the counter, spreading the plastic wrap back over it and replacing the note on top with a drawing of a smiling face.

XV.

It's not simply the newness of sensations. She feels them differently.

The shower is like rain.

It's something I've felt many times before, but this feels like the
first time. The warm droplets heat my skin.

For a moment, I simply let the water run over my host and me.

I'm completely unclothed. The warm water covering my body
feels incredible.

Showers are at the top of the list of things I like so far.

As I run her hands along my host's body, I discover that touching my own body produces pleasurable feelings. The amount of
pleasure seemingly corresponds to the area of my body I touch.

Something I'll have to explore later.

Pain.

Sharp pain stings as I move her hand through a tangle of hair. I
decide to leave her hair alone.

I start exploring the shower paraphernalia.

The soaps, shampoos and conditioners smell incredible. In each, I can pick out a tiny part of my host's scent. The loofah feels nice against her body, and the lather of soap it produces is fun to play with.

I don't want it to end.

But there's something else I'm curious about: the towel. From the information my host relays, I can see I'm supposed to use it to dry myself before applying lotion.

To my eyes, it looks soft. Her memories tell me it's also warm.

I turn the water off.

I'm immediately rewarded when I reach for it. It is both of those things. It joins the list of things I like about the human experience.

The towel rises and falls down the tangle of human limbs and body parts.

I wonder what other human sensations are this pleasurable. How do I even start to identify them?

So far, I've just followed my host's intuition. Should I continue to do the same? What else does she do in a day?

Work.

Unclear. There are too many images and definitions to piece together exactly what that means, but I do know I have to go to a certain location at a certain time.

It appears as though I will need to dress for it, though. That doesn't seem worth it.

I'll enjoy drying and experiencing "lotion" first.

And then I'll decide how badly I want to experience this "work."

XVI.

Although I don't like the idea of being fully clothed, I've mostly compromised and donned the outfit my host laid out for two reasons: to experience "work" and to limit the interruption to my host's plans.

I'm still not sure what allows me to inhabit this host, but learning her schedule will make it easier for me to find her in the future.

I did not, however, wear the small, breast-covering undergarment she laid out as it was too uncomfortable.

I steer my host out the door and into the hallway.

Lock the door, her voice warns.

I do so more easily this time than when I fiddled with her key and lock, and I start my descent.

Or I would have, but the sight of the interior of her apartment falls away.

All her human senses do.

And suddenly, I'm floating in my natural form. My human eyes are replaced only by my limited "sight," which identifies her conscious energy as she continues down the stairs.

Why now?

I follow my host as she continues down the stairs, out the front door, and into the park beyond.

No conscious energy leaks from her. She is fully in control. She is awake.

I'm reminded of what the other of my kind had asked: "You don't know how much longer you have?"

Should I have known that this time would be shorter? How?

I'm missing something.

As I follow, I try to observe in every way I can.

What is it that I can't see?

XVII.

We aren't far from where she lives.

In one of those larger buildings crawling with humans.

The different colors and shapes of conscious energy practically
buzz with activity. With human eyes, each floor seems like a
hive of tiny offices and cubicles.

For the last hour, I've been learning—occupying every human
within range of my host and asking their inner voices as many
questions as I could.

I've learned more than a few things.

I've learned the building holds many businesses, but this floor,
the two below and the one above are dedicated to a company
called Vivre.

I've learned my host works for Vivre as a designer, and most
people here seem to have either a slightly positive opinion of her
or no opinion at all.

I've learned her name is Jeanne.

Through another's eyes, I was able to catch a glimpse of her. She
looks different when she's fully awake.

More rigid.

More serious.

Harder somehow.

I like her better when we're together.

I've also learned something else. About myself.

As I've moved between hosts, I've observed my boundary. Each time I occupy someone, my boundary expands, but not uniformly. Sometimes, it's more, and sometimes, it's less.

It's something I've never noticed before because of the pain.

The pain was preoccupying. And the relief of stopping it was so strong I never stopped to examine the changes.

But now, I can.

Because of that, I've been able to observe the humans around me more closely. I can see what they look like using my natural sight, how their conscious energy flows, and how that corresponds to the expansion of my boundary.

I'm beginning to understand how long I can occupy a host and how much conscious energy they'll allow me to siphon.

And it's giving me an idea.

XVIII.

It's a risk.

I don't even really know what I'm looking for.

When I met the other one. That one in the park. He left in this direction.

He said he'd come and find me later on. But why wait? Based on what I've learned, I should be able to find him. Or, if not him, another of a similar age. Another that could teach me what I want to know.

Buildings are smaller at this point, which will only help with what I'm attempting.

I fly past each of the six or seven-story buildings, scanning the conscious energy of the humans within. There's so much varia-tion! Humans who leak smaller quantities than I've ever noticed, some who leak more. But no one is on the same level as Jeanne.

But by paying attention to the plumes of their conscious energy, I can learn more about their quality as hosts.

The woman in her apartment is about to nod off to sleep. Not worth inhabiting. Her consciousness only lapses for a second or two at a time. And it won't be long before she's completely asleep and closed off.

The jogger below is worth inhabiting, even if it wouldn't last very long. Focused to the point of unconsciousness. Unless someone gets in his way or distracts him, he would supply a fair amount of conscious energy.

In the building below, amongst a crowd of people, is another very worthwhile man. Similar to Jeanne, but more unstable. His movements are similarly erratic. I think he might be like the older man from earlier. A drunk.

But right now, I'm not looking for a host. I'm looking for something else—or at least I think I am.

And within an hour, I see it.

Several plumes of strong conscious energy emanate from one building.

I fly around it twice, to be certain. It's low and squat. Tucked between a number of other buildings. And the activity I'm looking for is below ground. I wouldn't have noticed it if it weren't for the two sitting out front.

One is leaking more conscious energy than I've ever seen. More than Jeanne.

The other . . . I don't understand.

It both is and isn't leaking conscious energy. One second it is, one second it isn't. But the amount it's leaking is never large enough to bother inhabiting.

It's impossible to ignore. Unnatural.

The majority of the plumes come from below.

There's the behavior I was looking for: multiple hosts leaking enormous amounts of conscious energy, but never for long. Each one is occupied shortly after becoming "vacant."

And then there's that eerie feeling from the sky. I felt it the moment I flew close enough to the lower level. The feeling of another boundary. A larger boundary intersecting mine.

This is the place. What is the best way to enter?

Should I just enter one of the available hosts?

Low and slow, I hover towards the basement until a voice booms through my boundary.

OUT FRONT.

Loud. So loud. The voice shakes my nucleus.

I pull back sharply to above the building until I can no longer feel others intersecting me.

That voice was so different from the others in the sky. Not at all welcoming.

Aggressive.

Threatening.

What did it mean? Out front?

The two humans in front of the building?

One is still vacant. The other is still intermittently leaking a tiny contrail of conscious energy.

Should I inhabit the vacant one?

Why not? If nothing else, it will give me the conscious energy to get back to my host.

I dive into the vacant plume of conscious energy, wondering what experience waits.

I can't move.

I have control, but nothing responds when I try to move. I'm locked in place. I don't understand. Am I not connected?

Human vision comes into focus. I am connected. I can see the street. Passersby. The occasional car. The restaurants and stores across the street.

But I can't move. Not even the smallest amount. I can't even feel my appendages.

How?

Should I detach?

I feel for my host's inner voice. Attempting to extract answers from him.

No answer.

This feels dangerous. This shouldn't be possible. Is my host restrained? No. It's like control of the body has been disconnected from the host's mind. But that can't be possible. For a human to be locked in. To be trapped.

I don't like this. I should—

A hand comes into my area of sight and turns my chair. It belongs to a red-headed woman.

Middle-aged. Worn.

There's something familiar about her. A crooked smile plays at her lips.

"Ah . . . it's you." she says. "That was faster than I expected."

XIX.

"I'm a little disappointed. I thought the next time I saw you, you would be in the body of that woman."

She knows me?

"Still, if you found this place in your natural form, you've learned a lot in the span of a couple days. That's worthy of praise."

I can't speak.

The crooked smile widens. It knows I can't answer. It's enjoying this.

"Do you remember me?"

I don't. But the options are limited. It can only be the one I met yesterday. The crooked smile and look of amusement match, even if they are on a different face.

It waits a minute, still smiling.

"Maybe not. If you haven't learned how to speak the other way yet, then you may not be able to tell us apart."

The other way? Tell us apart? What does it mean? I can't move much less speak in this body.

The smile fades from her face as she looks deeper into my host's eyes.

Here's a hint.

The words bounce around inside me. Not in my host's ears but inside my form. What was that?

That wasn't human speech. It spoke to me the same way the one below had before. The same way the ones in the sky did. But it never left its host. How is that possible?

If you can't figure it out on your own, the voice continues, *bring your host and I'll teach you this and more. In the meantime, you can use our recharging station free of charge.*

Alongside the last words, it points towards the human I'm inhabiting and laughs before leaving me staring at an empty chair.

XX.

There's so much I don't know.

Their voices echo in the back of my thoughts: *You probably don't know . . . You can't speak yet? Young one . . .*

I should be happy.

My boundary dances far beyond me. There's no pain. I'm able to explore an expanse of sky far beyond the city, the scurrying of humans, and the screams of my less fortunate kindreds.

Does the rest matter? Do I need to know?

I'm free.

At least freer than I've ever been. Free to explore and fly in my natural form for longer than I thought possible. Free to explore the human experience when I inhabit Jeanne.

Flashes of last night pass through me. The food. The feel of the shower. The towel.

What more could there be?

Bring your host and I'll teach you this and more.

My boundary falls with me as I fly lower. I can feel more as I expand: small tingles of pressure as I change elevations and speed, the warmth of conscious energy as humans, animals, and my own kind intersect me, and an expanded view of my surroundings.

As I focus on the park below, I can feel everything moving through it—a couple of viable hosts sit on nearby benches, conscious humans moving between the park and Jeanne.

It is her.

She's not leaking conscious energy, but I recognize the color of her consciousness. Her feel.

As she moves through the park, I follow. For some reason, I want to watch how her energy changes as she approaches her apartment building. Does she walk differently than I do in her form? Will she open the door the same way?

She stops.

Suddenly, her consciousness . . . it's leaking. Fascinating.

I don't need to feed right now.

I could leave her for one of my kind to occupy. I feel smaller, more desperate forms around me—like I used to be.

If they just knew what was possible.

But what would they do?

What would happen if they left without knowing about the key and the door? Would she be able to get into the building without it? Where would they take her if they inhabited her?

Would they harm her?

I shouldn't leave her outside and exposed to just any of my kind.

$\mathcal{XXI}.$

She's tired. Heavier than last time.

I finish turning the key to undo the lock, stepping into the warmth of the lobby.

Her feet drag as I do the slow walk up the stairs, down the hallway and to the door of her apartment.

Another lock. I mimic her movement from earlier, graceful and smooth, manipulating the key into the lock. Then, I gently turn the knob and step into the apartment as I close the door behind me.

My pride in the movements I completed spreads to her face and I feel a smile crack her lips.

Now what?

Should I leave her now? It will be a while until she's conscious again to see if my observation is correct. Plenty of time for another of my kind to grow their boundary significantly.

A cluster of pink down the hallway catches my eye and I find myself steering down towards the familiar desk. More Post-it notes?

Beside the smiling face from yesterday are two new notes: "Don't forget to eat!" and "Need to replace prescription." Under the second note, in smaller text, she's scrawled, "It's working!" with another smiling face.

The second one doesn't mean much to me, but I could do the first . . . and it would be another chance to experience eating.

I strip off her jacket and several of her bulkier clothing items. If I'm going to stay in her body for a little while, I may as well enjoy it.

I make my way to the kitchen, the cold floor tickling my feet. It's so much better this way.

The cold is unpleasant. I close the door. I don't want to eat something cold. I want something warm, like oatmeal. This morning, I used the small box—the microwave—to heat the food. Is there something I can heat the same way?

In the freezer. Pizza.

Interesting. I don't really understand the picture in my mind. But I want to try it.

I open an even colder part of the fridge. Horrible. I can't close it quick enough. But I manage to pull the cold circle of pizza from it before it closes.

Jeanne's dormant voice interprets the instructions in slow succession for me. I put the circle into the microwave, and enter in the correct time. The machine whirs to life.

I ease myself down onto the large chair. The softness of the cushions brushes my exposed skin, and I feel a smile form on my lips again. It's a welcome feeling—both the softness and the release of weight on my feet as I left them off the ground.

The smile stays with me as I look around the apartment. It's still how I left it. Clean. Bright. Colorful. Somehow reflecting the softness of my host.

The image of the rumpled clothes I left on the ground cuts my smile short. I check the time remaining on the microwave.

Enough time to fix it.

The cold tickles my feet and my legs complain as I stand again.

In the hallway, I reach down and pick up the pile of clothes and take them to their proper place. The now familiar voice guides me through hanging the jacket on a "clothes hanger."

Before I'm able to throw the remainder of the clothes in the bin my host defines as a "hamper," something falls.

The bottle from before. Pills. It's nearly empty now, though.

My prescription, my host's voice says, and the image of the Post-it note reappears in my mind.

Her brain interprets writing again as I look at the bottle. Sleeping pills. With a warning: "These pills may cause drowsiness, sleepwalking, and sleep paralysis."

Jeanne's voice explains all the terms in succession and I can't move from where I'm rooted. I turn the bottle and read the terms over, listening to the explanations again.

The explanations begin to explain two mysteries I had been contemplating. If I understand correctly, I believe these pills are responsible for my host's receptiveness to occupation. And I'm certain paralysis is what I experienced earlier today.

But I still don't completely understand how. I want to learn more. How can I?

Computer. Internet. Search.

The wave of words and images is hard to understand. But the first step seems to be to turn on a device with a screen in the larger room.

The microwave chime breaks my train of thought. My food is ready.

The computer can wait.

The smell of the pizza is intoxicating, and it drags a smile back onto my face. Before I can reach in to grab a piece, two of my host's memories float to the surface—strong memories of pain, both inside her mouth and at the tips of her fingers.

Burns? I look at her finger and there's a discoloration. A scar, her memory tells me.

I'll wait. I pull up a stool in front of the counter.

After a few minutes of staring at the pizza I can't wait any longer. I pick a slice and take a bite.

Laughter falls out of me as I reach for a second slice.

XXII.

Pain radiates through my stomach.

In a distant voice, Jeanne explains that I ate too much.

I disagree.

I would still be eating now if there had been more pizza in the freezer.

My sight travels from the computer screen in front of me to the open, now empty microwave across the room. Quiet fills the apartment. How long have I been absorbed in this machine?

A bit of pain shoots up my leg.

A cramp, her voice tells me. I haven't moved enough. Your human bodies require so much maintenance.

It does seem like a waste.

I've never been in a body this long. Hours. And for most of the time, I've been completely immobile. Staring at this screen.

But the things I've learned.

This world is so much larger than I ever knew.

This city is such a small portion of it. What else is out there?

What other types of humans exist? What other types of my own kind? What other creatures?

It seems humans are only aware of creatures that are visible to them, either through their human eyes or using machines to increase their vision. This is a very limited and narrow understanding of the world, but I suppose I am not one to judge, given how little I knew only days ago.

I glance over at the bit of text in a small window I've kept open for some time. My host's voice translates it for the near hundredth time.

Fugue state: a temporary state where a human experiences memory loss. After which they may end up somewhere without knowing how they got there.

No mention of leaking consciousness. But it explains the state viable human hosts enter perfectly.

From my time sifting through information on this "Internet" (something I still don't completely understand and I'm not sure my host does either), it seems like many things can put humans in a fugue state: substances, injuries, events.

In my host's case, it's likely related to the pills I found earlier. But it's not their main effect. And Jeanne may not be fully aware of the full effect.

I glance at the Post-it note from earlier, reminding her to refill the subscription. Warmth fills me when I see the smiling face. Whether she's aware of the full effect or not, my host seems as happy with our situation as I am.

My body lulls and my eyes flicker.

She's weary. But I don't feel her sleep coming. From my estimation, she will remain in this "fugue" state for several more hours.

I pick up the pill bottle and roll it between my host's fingers. I take two as instructed on the package.

Jeanne's health is essential for our arrangement to continue to work. And these pills are the cornerstone of that. If they stop working, she may stop taking them.

I shudder at the thought of being without her. Of going back to the drunks. Or worse, those without control at all.

This relationship must continue, and each of us must contribute to the health of the other.

A mutually beneficial relationship. But also a necessary one.

Symbiotic, Jeanne says quietly from beneath, supplying an answer to a question she must have thought I was asking.

Her definition is unclear. I use the computer to search for the term.

"A mutually beneficial relationship between one or more groups and/or people."

Yes. Exactly!

Understanding suddenly washes over me.

I leap from Jeanne and begin to ascend.

XXIII.

I've never moved this fast.

I had expected to slow with size, but the expansion of my boundary has not changed my mobility at all. I still float, and my boundary still dances—it simply does so over a larger area.

My size is difficult for me to believe. I still pale in comparison to the one from before. From the ones above. The ones I'm flying directly towards.

Young one, I remember them calling me.

Not anymore. Not for long.

I can feel more at this size. The air gets colder as my formless mass rises.

It's not the same as when I'm in my human body. Cold isn't uncomfortable. It's recognizable but not painful. It slows me, increasing the rigidity of my boundary. It dances to a different rhythm as I ascend higher. Staccato movements following each other.

My boundary intersects something unbelievably large and I know I'm here.

You're back, young one, its voice speaks into me.

Curious. Amused.

I had forgotten about this part. I still don't know how to speak.

Something like laughter reverberates around me. Not unkind. Incredulous but still without rebuke.

You still cannot speak?

How do I do it?

It may still be too early for you. You should stop rising. Before . . .

I don't hear the rest. I feel the pull again. As expected, my boundary starts to recede. Not quickly. I'm in no immediate danger at my size. And I don't stop rising. Not when I'm so close to understanding.

I focus on the edges of my boundary, trying to understand how my conscious energy is being siphoned.

What are you attempting, young one?

The voice is filled with curiosity.

If I teach you to speak, will you tell me? it asks.

Yes!

It doesn't hear me.

Hmm, it muses. *I suppose you can't answer to make the deal.*

Yes! It's a deal!

A pity . . . you'll fade into nothing, and I'll never know.

TEACH ME! I scream, pushing the frustration and desperation through my form as broadly as I can.

Laughter booms into me.

It heard me.

I focus on how I had projected that thought. It reverberated through me and outwards, vibrating out to my boundary and back.

I've fulfilled my part of the bargain, young one. Tell me what you are doing before you fade away. Feel what you want to say and push it through to your boundary.

You live through the symbiotic sharing of conscious energy, I assert with some difficulty. *How?*

No answer.

It didn't work. I need to hurry. My boundary is shrinking faster now. I'm still not in danger, but cannot stay here much longer.

HOW DO YOU SHARE ENERGY? I scream.

I can feel the others considering. There are multiple of my kind intersecting me now. They're impossibly expansive. Their voices echo in their vastness.

In the same way you feed on human consciousness, one answers casually.

I don't understand. How I feed on human consciousness? I simply do. It's not something I do purposely.

Fly lower, young one, the original one says softly. *Sharing with only one of us will allow you more time to understand.*

They're right. At this rate, I would be burned out of existence in mere hours. I need to lower myself.

As I do, I feel the other boundaries move away, their curiosity and interest waning as they move away. They are not uncaring.

But they acquiesce to the one I had originally spoken to.

Once I'm low enough, the siphoning of my energy slows considerably.

You can stay as long as you wish, but I cannot stop or slow the rate at which I draw energy from you, the voice warns. *Nor can I explain how I do so. It is an automatic function for me.*

Thank you, I struggle to communicate. I feel the gratitude reverberate along my form.

It hears but does not answer. A sort of warmth rises in me as it passes feelings of empathy and something else. Pity.

It was once like me. It understands my want.

I focus on the feeling of conscious energy drawing from me. Trying to entrain the feeling in me. Trying to understand how it works. Trying to trigger the same in myself.

I lose myself in the feeling.

I lose the concept of time in the effort.

You do not have much more time, young one, the voice warns after some time.

The voice pulls me back. I can feel sunlight brightening my form. How long have I been lost?

My boundary is pulled so close.

Prickling. Not pain quite yet, but it won't be long.

But I think I understand now.

My boundary ripples and opens.

I've never thought of it as open or closed before, but it is. With my boundary open, I can feel conscious energy flowing into me. With it closed, not only can I not feel energy, but the siphoning seems to stop.

I toy around with opening it in specific places. In some, it pulls at the conscious energy through the intersection points with the much larger entity.

A slow relief trickles into me.

A low rumble of satisfaction flows out of my senior.

My understanding of my boundary helps me speak with less effort. I let my thoughts and feelings flow out where my boundary opens.

You are very welcome, young one, the voice answers, *but you must still improve. You are not pulling energy from me at an equal rate.*

I'm aware of its correctness as soon as it says it. My boundary is still slowly receding. Barely perceptible, but it is still shrinking.

Return when you can do so safely, it says sincerely as it pulls away, rising into the shared mass of the others.

I begin my descent.

The prickling of my boundary is overwhelmed by the awe and satisfaction of what I've learned.

In those moments, my boundary was open, and I felt much more connected. I could feel more of what my elder was, what it had experienced, its age, the knowledge it had amassed, and its true size.

I would have thought it was impossible for one of us to be so much.

But now I know I can be more as well.

XXIV.

It will take me some time to return to a safe size.

Longer to reach a size worthy of approaching those elders again.

In the meantime, I've decided to stay close to Jeanne, inhabiting anyone who crosses my path in the process.

My boundary has changed.

Or maybe my new understanding of it has just made me aware of its nuances.

I've experimented with opening it wider. Closing it tighter.

With it open, I draw in more conscious energy from the humans I inhabit. With it closed, I leak less conscious energy into my natural form. Closing it also offers me a respite from the screams of my kind unraveling.

I accidentally open my boundary too wide as I intersect another of my kind. I feel its panic. It's too small and I've inadvertently stolen precious life force from it.

I immediately close my boundary. I feel it scream as the pain intensifies. It flits towards the closest host.

I must be more careful.

While I haven't felt that panic in days, it's still all too real for others.

In shame, I raise myself further from the ground as I continue to experiment with my boundary further away from where the humans and the younger ones of my kind rest.

Jeanne's color changes slightly ahead of me.

It's midday, and her conscious energy begins to leak for the first time today from her position at her workplace. Her head doesn't drop, and her body doesn't change. Looking at her through human eyes, there's probably no change. But her consciousness is fading fast.

I take advantage of the opportunity to occupy her and recharge my depleted energy.

Conscious energy floods into me as I open my boundary to receive it. Then her consciousness gives way completely, and control of the body passes to me.

There's a screen in front of me. Images and text.

Work, her voice informs me.

The description implies that "work" is necessary for her survival. But there is another thing—a conflict. Work is both the thing that will allow her to travel and the reason she can't.

Hard to understand.

Her inner voice tries to explain further and I grasp the concept of "time off." Following Jeanne's slumbering guidance I locate a request form for "vacation" and submit a request for a month from now.

The importance of Jeanne's "work" is clear, but so is her desire for travel.

So I'll help her with both.

Symbiotic.

I smile as I turn my attention to her task at hand.

What was she working on?

A presentation.

Her voice answers, and I can see a slightly different version of it in her mind—a more complete version and a road map to get there.

I move my hand and the mouse in my grip follows her directions.

I click. I drag. I position.

Colorful boxes and lines follow my keystrokes and the presentation in front of me slowly becomes the one in her mind.

Ingenious.

These devices you humans create to bring what is in your mind into the real world shows how concerned you are with sharing that information with others.

"You want to grab a coffee?"

I'm broken out of my fascination by another human. Taller. Larger. Decidedly hairier and more angled.

Before I can say anything, I'm ejected from my host and floating in between.

Jeanne's consciousness must have returned.

I was careless.

I hadn't been paying attention to how close to the surface she had been.

Still, even in that small occupation, I expanded sizeably. My boundary no longer hangs cloyingly close. No prickles or pain.

I float nearby and follow my host as she follows the other human.

Nearby, another human begins to leak consciousness, and I take the opportunity to occupy them.

Unhelpful.

I have no control. To make matters worse, this one is staring at a table. I can vaguely hear her speaking across the room, but I can't observe them.

Or can I?

I am larger now than the vacancy my current host offers—a shallow vagueness if I were evaluating it. At most, another minute and my host will snap back from his place slightly below the surface.

Because of the limit, I can feel my boundary floating beyond the host. I detach myself partially. I let my boundary open enough to siphon energy from this host. I keep the rest of my boundary closed to ensure no other of my kind can take my place.

I straddle the strange feeling of being both within this body and not.

I can vaguely feel the warmth of the room. My host's elbow against the table. The curve of the chair behind me.

But I can also feel my boundary and see the world as I do in my native form, feeling consciousness and energy.

I remember how the one from earlier was able to speak to my natural form as it occupied a host.

This is how they did it!

In my excitement, I lose the connection to the current host.

It's difficult, like looking in two directions in a human body. It doesn't feel natural.

But if I can do this, what else can I do?

I leave Jeanne and her coworkers behind in search of hosts to use for practice.

XXV.

It hasn't gotten easier.

Even with hours of practice I've only managed to hold a connection with a host for around a minute while maintaining awareness of my natural form.

The one from earlier. I can't help but be awed by its skill and control.

Imagine.

Not only being able to hold that duality but also being able to speak.

How old must that one be?

As old as the ones above?

For that matter, why isn't it with the ones above?

Bring your host, it had said.

I will.

XXVI.

Finally.

After following her around to her workplace and back, she's finally entered a fugue state.

I stretch her arms and legs.

It's comfortable in this bed. Under the covers. Warm.

I almost don't want to leave, but I have so much time remaining. She's deep beneath the surface.

And I have so much to do.

The cold floor is deeply unpleasant as I step out of bed. I must find clothing quickly. Luckily, there's some on the floor nearby.

I frown as I look at the mess Jeanne has generated in the past few hours. She has nearly undone the cleaning I had done the night prior. But there's no time to dwell on that.

I need to figure out how to get back there. I had flown earlier. I know the direction, but how far?

And what would be the fastest way to get there in this body?

The train.

Her voice is so quiet. Barely audible beneath the veil of consciousness. Barely filling in the details of what the train is or where to catch it.

But I don't need her for that. The Internet can answer this question. It can tell me the where and how as long as I know the what.

In minutes, I have those answers.

Soon, I'm out the door and on my way to search for more.

XXVII.

I'm careful not to lose my connection as I split my form between Jeanne and myself, searching for the cluster of conscious energy.

It took about an hour to find the train, ride from station to station, and spot a familiar neighborhood as we sped past on the elevated rail. I wandered around the neighborhood until I found the building I was looking for.

Jeanne hasn't changed since I left. She is still slumbering so deep below the surface that I can barely feel her. Her calm slumber is a sharp contrast to the nervous excitement I feel.

The feeling, I assume, is responsible for the pimpling of my skin.

This is it.

If I hadn't recognized it, the lone figure sitting on the porch would have given it away. Unmoving.

Impossibly still.

As I come up the stairs, I notice the eyes. Unblinking. And the bags of fluid running into him through tiny tubes.

The chair across from him is empty.

"Can I help you?"

A familiar face pokes out the front door. Not the lady from last time. The young man I met in the park.

It takes almost all my concentration to split myself. I had practiced this on the train.

I learned. I project across my boundary.

"You must be looking for Hobbes," he smiles. "One second."

The door shuts and almost immediately opens again.

The face that opens it is larger and darker. A crooked smile hangs below sunken eyes.

"Ah, it's you," it says, unsurprised.

How many hosts does it have?

You said to come visit when I was in this form, I force through my boundary, a little embarrassed to be doing it a second time.

The dark man whistles. Surprised.

"Quick learner, aren't you?"

Before I can answer, it smiles wider and opens the door.

"I'm glad you've come. Come on in. I'll show you around," it laughs and gestures for me to go inside but stops as he catches my eyes lingering on the still human seated on the porch.

"That's the one you inhabited on your last visit."

"What's wrong with him?" I ask before I can think of a better question. Looking at him is uncomfortable. He looks wrong.

"He's what humans call a 'vegetable,'" it explains. "No identity of his own, but still alive. Still conscious. An empty shell."

"How does that happen?"

It raises an extremely large hand to its chin to ponder. There is a hint of pride in its voice.

"A number of ways. This particular one was in a car accident before we bought him. We have another who is medically induced. They make great recharging stations."

My eyes travel along the vegetable's form, and I remember being trapped in that body. Now that I can split myself between my host and natural state, it seems less frightening but certainly not comfortable.

A small mercy for the humans, maybe, if their consciousness is truly gone.

"The rest are down here."

Its voice snaps me out of my thoughts. The inside of the house is featureless. It is smaller and cleaner than the lobby of Jeanne's building, and it is more similar to the inside of the apartment. It has white walls and dark, flat floors, but without the accompaniment of the colors and textures of Jeanne's fabrics.

A curved staircase leads down. The bottom is not immediately visible from the top.

"Do you have a name?" it asks.

"A name?" I exhale. I wasn't prepared. It takes me time to regain my breath. "Like my host's?"

"No," it says, laughing again at my confusion.

Slightly unkind. Teasing.

"Your own," it clarifies. "I suppose most don't when they come here. It's not in some of our natures, maybe. To be an individual."

It stops a step below me to turn and offer its hand.

"But I am. And I'm Hobbes."

Shake it. A distant Jeanne says. Teaching me how.

He leads me further down the stairs, and after what seems like a full turnaround, the end finally becomes visible.

At the bottom, a small standing room greets us. In it, a single human (the one who answered the door) waits in front of yet another door.

Large and heavy.

At least compared to the doorways I've seen.

A pleasant old wood grain.

Similar to the lobby of Jeanne's home.

Hobbes opens the door and walks into the dark room beyond.

I follow.

XXVIII.

A sweet smell.

While my eyes adjust to the dimness of the room beyond, I focus on my host's other senses.

Warmth. And quiet.

But also not.

The low-level hum of the city disappears as the door falls into place behind us. But under the veil of quietness, I begin to hear soft music and human voices.

Not words.

Moans, Jeanne identifies. The pictures that come with it make me shudder.

A tangling of human bodies.

Too close for comfort.

My eyes adjust and the room's enormity comes into focus.

The floor is completely covered in various types of carpet and cushions, many with long, soft strings reaching up. Candles maintain a baseline of light throughout, and art covers every wall.

Pictures of tangling human bodies come into life around me.

There are so many of them.

They are strewn about the room, engaging in what Jeanne defines as sex, although there seem to be other words and names associated with the specific acts.

"It's a lot to take in, isn't it?"

Hobbes smiles proudly beside me. His eyes are waiting for my reaction.

"Why?" is the question I settle on.

This makes him erupt with laughter. While he recovers, I explore the room with my eyes.

There are tables of food and drinks, more art and sculptures around the room, and bowls of small things, like what Jeanne holds in the small bottle—pills.

"Because of how it feels," Hobbes explains after he stops laughing. "But it isn't just sex. That's obviously one of the most engaging activities, but it's only a part of what we do here."

He points around the room.

"The finest foods to experience," he narrates. "A variety of art and sculpture both to enjoy and emulate. And a plethora of drugs to experiment with in order to keep our hosts in a 'receptive' state."

"You can keep hosts in a fugue state?" I ask.

"Somewhat. Not forever, but certainly for a while," he explains as he leads me deeper into the room. "Humans need to sleep to recover, so we need to factor that in. What drugs does your host use?"

Impressive.

He smiles knowingly, and I pull the pill bottle out of my host's purse and hand it to Hobbes. He rolls it in his hand and nods.

"Sleeping pills," he says. "Common, but not terribly reliable. The effects are only helpful if your host is abusing them . . . which thankfully she must be."

He reaches out and grabs a few pills out of a nearby bowl.

"These," he smiles, "will almost immediately put her into a 'receptive' state lasting for a few hours."

"Will she notice?" I ask, rolling the pills in my hand.

"Does that matter?"

Symbiotic. I remember the word as I contemplate the question. A flash of Jeanne's smiling face appears in my mind.

"If she notices," I explain, "then she may take countermeasures, making her less receptive."

The room expands out to the side, and Hobbes points out a number of prone bodies on the ground.

"Ideally, she wouldn't have the chance," he says. "We try to keep hosts here as much as possible. It's one of the reasons we require all of our members to bring at least one host. We can then share and swap as they rest."

"You share hosts?"

It's obvious as soon as the words slip out of me.

Hobbes' brow raises at the question.

"Of course," he says, confused. "They're just hosts. Do you only occupy that one?"

"Of course not," I say. My cheeks burn.

The crooked smile reappears on his face, and Hobbes claps my shoulder.

"Don't worry about it; we're all attached to our firsts," he tells me.

"What else do you have here?" I ask, trying to change the subject and stop my cheeks from burning.

"Showers," he says, pointing to a set of doors at the back of the room. "Washrooms, obviously. A couple more 'charging stations' similar to the one upstairs."

"Nice body!"

A larger human interrupts us and stares me up and down. The hairs on my arms raise and I feel something inside myself shake. An automatic function of this body?

You're new, aren't you? I hear reverberate across my boundary. It's not a natural voice.

Choppy. Unpracticed.

I am, I answer in kind, feeling its size through my open boundary.

It's small.

I'm surprised.

Hobbes is so expansive and old, as was the other I came into contact with the last time I was here. I had expected the rest of the members to be equally so.

But this one is smaller than I am by a considerable margin.

"What do you think? Do you want to learn more?" Hobbes asks, watching me stare at the other.

The larger man doesn't entice me.

Hobbes nods in the direction of a nearby tangle of bodies.

"You'll be surprised by what your body can feel," he promises.

I feel for Jeanne. Still deep beneath the surface. Still plenty of time.

"Sure," I hear roll out of my mouth. "Teach me."

XXIX.

Something stirs just beneath the surface.

Jeanne.

I can feel her starting to wake up.

"Do you want to try out this one?" Hobbes asks, running my hand along the sinew of his current host's body. "We could switch."

My breath is still caught in my chest. My mind is still full of the sensations of the past hour.

But that snaps me out of it.

"No."

It comes out of my mouth far more quickly and forcefully than I meant to say it. Hobbes is unsurprised. But the others shift their attention at the change in my voice.

"I can feel her starting to wake," I correct. "I should go."

Hobbes smiles and separates from the tangle with me.

"Take one of the blue ones. It will put her to sleep and then you can swap into another body."

He points to a nearby bowl of pills. His smile stays on his face, but its warmth fades.

He's testing me.

"Not today," I say, looking for my clothes. "I would like to learn more about my host and this world."

"I can teach you more about this world," he says, a bit of warmth returning. "We don't need to stay here. Let her rest and we can wander around the neighborhood."

I wander farther from the tangle and begin to dress.

"Another time," I say, wondering if I mean it.

XXX.

It's late by the time I open the door of the apartment.

Thankfully, Jeanne stayed below the surface the entire way home. A few times, I thought she would wake and I would be flung out of her body. But she sank back below each time she came close to breaching the surface. Not far, just deep enough to keep me in control.

Even now I can feel her. She's both close to waking and not.

Her body is equally close to sleeping.

It's heavy. Weary.

Complete unconsciousness is probably what it's craving.

Shower.

Very faintly, I hear her voice as I creep towards her bed.

I look at us in a nearby mirror—our body.

Her body.

Symbiotic. I remember.

Yes. I should clean it before it's returned to her control.

I remember the mess I had seen when I left.

I should clean that, too.

XXXI.

Dancing.

From my core to my boundary, my natural form falls in line with the lead of a late-night gust.

The gust takes me into the city beneath—between buildings, in and out of open windows, under bridges.

The wind carries me into a crowd and I feel several of my own kind intersect me.

So small. So young.

So many.

I hadn't noticed how many receptive humans were around. Another gust plucks me from the crowd and leads me down the street. Several more of my kind intersect me and several more receptive humans radiate conscious energy around me.

Out of curiosity, I inhabit one.

My "sight" is replaced by the view out of a small man's eyes. Low to the ground for man. Around me, fancily dressed women and men crowd around the entrance of a building.

Club, a gargled voice defines from beneath the surface. And I realize suddenly I have complete control of his form.

And I recognize why.

Dizziness in my eyes and uncertain balance. The slight feeling of sickness in my stomach. And the recognizable taste of alcohol.

I leave my uncomfortable host behind and float around the area. I open my boundary for a second, feeling how many of my own kind are around.

There were as many as I had thought. But with my boundary, I can feel the variety of their sizes. None of them rivals my size, but so many are larger than I was at my smallest.

I can see them flicker in and out of sight as they inhabit nearby hosts. Closing their boundaries either on purpose or because they have not yet learned to keep them open at the same time.

They'll learn in time.

Something nips at my conscious energy and I close my boundary on reflex. The drain does not disappear. I feel a pull on my closed boundary.

Strong. Hostile.

I let another gust take me away. The drain stops.

What was that?

The gust carries me into a nearby window, and another curiosity invades my thoughts. In front of me, two conscious energies intertwine. One unreceptive human moves above another, whose consciousness leaks slightly.

The movements above the energy remind me of earlier in my evening.

Slow. Rhythmic.

Curiosity wins and I leap into the bottom-most human. Her feelings slowly become mine.

Sex.

Above me her partner glistens with sweat. I can feel a sort of dull almost-pleasure from where we connect. It's similar to what I experienced earlier. But less.

I don't have control. My host's consciousness has not given way completely. But I can feel the heat of our bodies. The roughness of his body hair. Short bursts of breath as his movements pick up.

The almost-pleasure lessens.

Even so, I'm surprised that human consciousness could lapse under this circumstance. Memories of earlier in my evening flow through me and I frown at this host's meager sensations.

"Does it feel good for you?"

A tentative voice in between blasts of breath.

And I'm out.

Back in my natural form.

The two energies in front of me are still intertwined, but with my former host fully in control.

I float through the barriers of the building's walls and back into the night sky. The gown of my boundary follows behind me—a smooth arc as I lance further into the darkness above the city lights.

My thoughts drift back to Jeanne.

She's different. The sensations in her body are better. None of the dizziness of drunks. None of the indifference of others.

Always strong and pleasurable sensations.

I turn in the sky as I consider how late I kept her out.

Symbiotic, the word rings in my head.

A promise. A warning.

I think of Jeanne's board. Her notes. Her smiling faces.

Symbiotic.

I think of all the sensations of the previous night.

Symbiotic.

I think of how I can help her experience the things she wants in return.

XXXII.

I want to see her when she wakes up.

Her conscious energy hasn't changed yet.

Slow. Quiet. Flat.

Asleep.

It would be helpful to see her through human eyes, to read her expressions, movements, and emotional state.

I wonder again if she would have enjoyed the events of the previous night had she been awake. She is adventurous. Or at least she endeavors to be when work isn't in the way. And the way it felt. Surely, she would have appreciated—

She's stirring.

The slow, flat energy gives way to a pulse of quick, frantic energy. Has she noticed something?

She's moving. Quickly. Around the apartment and towards the door.

I wish I could see her.

I fly through the walls. Out in front. Down to the park.

There has to be someone. At this hour, there should be plenty of options.

There!

Someone moving in the opposite direction. A shallow connection, but it should give me a glimpse.

I open a portion of my boundary. Just enough to take what I need.

The dim glow of morning and the green of the park beyond snap into focus. Ahead, a street and the entrance to a building.

She's there.

Jeanne exits the building in the outfit I laid out after my shower. Her face is out of focus. This host's vision is poorer than I'm used to, but that should only be an issue for a little longer.

She's moving quicker than normal. And she's distracted. Head low.

Does she know? I knew last night was a mistake.

She's getting closer and her features begin to focus. Her brow is furrowed. A muscle twitches at the side of her jaw.

Something is wrong.

And she's not paying attention to this person coming at her. At this rate, she's going to collide with him. I'll lose my connection to this host if he's startled.

I open my boundary and inhabit the nearest person I can.

They collide.

I can't see it. This host is staring at the ground. And I have no control.

Damn!

"Sorry, I'm very late for work," I hear from beyond this person's periphery.

And suddenly, I'm disconnected. Cut off from human sensation and floating in my natural form.

I can sense Jeanne's energy continuing in her original direction, but I don't need to follow her anymore.

Not immediately.

My boundary pulses. An exhale of tension. The cause of her distress has nothing to do with the events of last night.

How funny your human relationship with time is. It seems to pass with much more urgency and consequence. Without the pressure of my boundary dissolving and the pain that comes with it, the passage of time barely registers to me.

For just a second, my boundary intersects with another of my kind.

So small. So frail.

As I used to be.

A thought occurs to me.

I open my boundary and attempt to push energy away from me. To share in some small part what I've been fortunate enough to gain.

No energy leaves me. This one's boundary is closed. A shame.

I watch the various shapes and movements of conscious energy around me.

Are there as many of us as there are humans? Do we exist in the same variety? Milling around on our way from one thing to another? Some struggling to merely survive, others . . .

What are others doing?

Those like me who no longer struggle to survive. What are they doing? Do they fly around like me? Free and aimless.

Not Hobbes, I suppose.

My boundary dances with memories of what I experienced the previous night. Sensations that I could never have experienced in my own form.

Smells. Touches. Release.

There are worse things to pursue.

And yet still, there's . . . something. Something hard to describe. Not a thought. Not a feeling.

Something.

Another small one passes through my boundary. This one is smart enough to take advantage of the aid I offer. It is not young. I can feel its age and experience through our exchange of energy. It is not young but still naïve to life beyond the struggle for survival.

Some humans will sustain you better than others. Learn to read the differences in their conscious energy.

It is the most helpful advice I can think to impart.

It closes its boundary, shooting away with fearful haste.

It must not have learned how to speak yet. I hope it still considers what I said after the shock wears off.

Perhaps I should have told it about Hobbes.

Or the elder ones above.

I strain to feel their presence.

They're there. In the same place.

No.

They've moved. Only slightly.

But if I compare where I met them the last few times they are moving.

In a single direction. Slowly but intentionally.

Where are they going?

XXXIII.

You've regained your size, young one.

They're not surprised.

But the rumbling echo of their voices reverberates with a sort of dull amusement.

Have you come to join us?

I'm not sure how to answer the question. I hadn't considered joining them.

I can feel the others' curiosity pique.

As they crowd around, it takes me some time to calibrate my boundary to intake as much energy as is being drained from me. It's an odd feeling—a sort of stasis.

My boundary no longer recedes. But neither does it grow.

You've become more adept, one compliments. A different voice, but not at the same time.

They're speaking as one.

They begin to push thoughts across my boundary. They are explanations of the kind only we can give—not words or images but sensations, memories, and knowledge.

What does joining you mean?

I've begun to understand that I'm stalling. A shudder threatens to throw off the careful balance or energy transfer I'm maintaining. I struggle to bring it back in line.

You are experiencing it, a chorus of voices confirm. *We are one and multiple. Free from any threat of dissolution. Free from a need for hosts.*

My stomach churns at their use of the word free.

You never take hosts? I ask, realizing the implication. Snippets of my time with Hobbes slip through my boundary.

I feel some recoil at my memories.

Not disgust. Not from all of them.

Hurt. Longing. Fear mingled with a distant fondness.

Most of us who had any attachment to the human form have outgrown it, a voice rumbles, speaking for them. *For those of us who haven't, we can experience the sensations of humanity through our shared experience and memory.*

Feelings and memories flow through my boundary. I feel them as if they're real. The smell of a city long ago. The feeling of feet against the sand of a beach.

At the same time, I feel the tickle of cold, the expansion of warmth, the dancing of boundaries in unison—sensations that can only be experienced in our natural state. I feel free and content. I see the expanse of the sky as seen from their perspective.

Where are you going?

The question that brought me here.

No single voice answers. They project as one into me.

Impossible things. Beautiful things.

Expanses of water that are unbelievably large. Impossibly different landscapes. Varieties of humans I've never seen.

I feel them riding the wind. There is no single answer to my question. They are not going anywhere. They are freely following whatever wind chooses them. More will join them, and with each new joining, they will be shown secrets of the world most of my kind will never see.

One last feeling passes through their boundaries. A feeling so familiar for a second I'm not sure it doesn't belong to me.

The in-between. The joy. The pure enjoyment of being in this natural state of ours. The feeling of a boundary dancing.

All of that is real? I feel myself ask.

There is a chorus of what I can only describe as laughter. Not unkind. Warm empathy from those who understand how it feels to finally understand the possible.

The world is larger than you can imagine, young one.

I parse through every bit of information they've shared with me. The collective's memories. The collective's experiences.

The collective.

The wave of revulsion from earlier courses through me.

You are conjoined?

The question is thrown from my boundary too sharply. Some wince at the accusation.

The truth.

We exist in symbiosis, the collective answers. *A small sacrifice to make for the freedom we are afforded.*

My boundary spreads to examine them with my new understanding.

As a result of keeping their barriers open for so long, they've become one.

They share thoughts. Ideas. Their whole existence.

It is not that they don't take hosts anymore. They can't. Many of them don't even remember how to separate themselves anymore. They're unable to close their boundaries, atrophied in place.

I shut my boundary in several places on reflex.

Not fast enough to stop the flow of information. Only now do I see what I didn't before: younger ones who have never experienced anything but memories of others. Regrets of ones who wish they could leave and can't—a symphony of feelings.

My revulsion flows up to them. Recent memories of my human experiences. The pure joy of flying alone, untethered in my moments in between.

Some try to shut me out but can't. An understanding, if disappointed voice flows into my boundary.

Do not pity us, it says more warmly than I deserve. *This is a choice we have made. And this method of survival affords us more freedom than most.*

And you are welcome to join us at any time.

The last part it says while fully understanding that I won't.

Thank you for all you have taught me, I answer, doing my best to hold back any judgment of what they've become. Instead, I push through honest gratitude, memories of what I was before I met them, and what I am now. I hope they'll understand how far they've allowed me to come.

And why I could never join them.

Be careful, young one, the last one warns me as it floats away. *The path you've chosen is a dangerous one.*

The connection breaks. And I'm left alone in the sky.

Untethered. Free. Boundary dancing in the cold altitude.

I watch the old ones, who cherish the same feelings I do, who have explored the corners of the world, who live in between.

I watch them fly off.

Unsure how I should move forward.

XXXIV.

I'm not going back to Jeanne.

Not right away.

Thoughts of the collective fill the shroud of my expanse.

Conjoined. Tangled. Stuck.

We exist in symbiosis, I hear one say again.

I shudder.

I will inhabit only myself until it is necessary to go back.

I try my best to shut out other thoughts, focusing on the space between my core and boundary and letting myself enjoy the expansion and contraction of my expanse.

For these moments, at least, I will feel only pride and joy in what I have become. I will compare myself only to what I was in the past. How much I have grown. How much I have learned.

I longed for this.

For the freedom of this form. Without pain and fear. Without the threat of dissolution.

And now that I have it, I will try my best to shut out other thoughts.

XXXV.

The cold air prickles against the small hairs on Jeanne's arms.

She must have forgotten a jacket in the rush this morning.

It's not altogether unpleasant, just another of the many sensations that make inhabiting this body fun. Beyond just the utility of charging. Which, if necessary, I could achieve using others.

Like Hobbes's recharging station, I think. My expanse shivers at the memory of paralysis.

Yes, like that but more fun. And if there were one that was more fun, I would . . .

What would I do?

Are there others that would be more fun?

I step off the sidewalk into a narrow garden alongside the building wall in front of me. Using the window wall in front of me, I examine Jeanne's unjacketed form, searching along the pleasantness of her amidst the scurrying crowds on the sidewalk behind us.

The soft skin and features, the colorful and tastefully contrasting T-shirt, pants and shoes, and the wavy hair leisurely swaying in the wind.

The other bodies I've experienced so far have only ever paled in comparison. However, from what Hobbes says, there are pleasures in each different body type that can be explored.

I take a close look at the larger woman passing me.

Powerful, longer limbs. More pronounced curves. Floral scented.

Certainly different.

Not in a bad way.

She passes me and grabs hold of a man.

Muscular. Intense smelling. Too precisely manicured.

Masculine.

If I think about it, the other hosts I've been able to fully control have been similarly masculine. I've assumed Jeanne is unique.

But maybe another more feminine host would be similar. Even superior.

I think of the disappointing sexual experience from my brief inhabitation last night.

Perhaps not.

It's not just her physical features.

Jeanne's body turns slightly in the reflection.

She's understated with betraying accents. The choice of bright but subdued colors. Slight tones of muscle. Trickles of adventure in her spirit.

I picture the locations from her board. Think of the vacation time I booked.

Symbiotic.

I smile to myself. For real. Not like those in the sky.

I wonder suddenly if Jeanne noticed I had booked the time off. If she had thought of which location she wanted to visit at all.

Cancelled. Her inner voice says softly.

A frown forms on Jeanne's reflection.

Why?

Thoughts and feelings in a jumble. Fear. Regret. A complex series of thoughts around job status. A promotion?

Jeanne's inner voice quiets.

The powerful limbed woman and her partner walk far ahead of me in the direction of Jeanne's apartment building.

I feel for Jeanne's consciousness, still calmly below the surface.

I won't go home just yet.

XXXVI.

"Look who's back."

Hobbes smiles at me from behind a dirty-blond mop of hair. Back in the body of the woman I had met previously. For the first time I notice how muscular she is. More muscular than Jeanne, but not by much.

But still in the direction of what I want.

"I would like to try another body," I say.

It sounds casual. Unpracticed.

It isn't.

She smiles and moves past me to sit on the porch, motioning to the chair beside the charging station.

"What changed your mind?" Hobbes asks, pulling out a small box.

Cigarettes, a sleepy Jeanne informs me.

"I was thinking about what you said about different sensations," I say, edging my chair as far away from the charging station as it can go.

She doesn't say anything. Her cigarette hangs in the crooked smile. Waiting for a light.

Her eyes are waiting for more information.

"I'm attached to this body," I answer, "but it's not me. When I'm not in my natural form, I want to be free to explore everything this world has to offer. Without restriction. Without dependence."

Hobbes taps ashes from her now-lit cigarette into a small bowl. Smoke escapes from a wider smile.

"You met them," she says, pointing skyward. It's not a question.

"I had met them before," I explain. "I didn't know how they . . . lived until recently."

She nods.

"You didn't consider joining them?" she asks. "You could have seen the world. Been free to fly on the wind for eternity." Hobbes's crooked smile relaxes. Her eyes probe me seriously. She's genuinely curious.

I shudder again at the thought of joining them.

"No."

An honest answer. Hobbes tilts her head, waiting for more.

"I like being Jeanne," I admit, uncomfortable with the admission. "Being human. Not as much as being in my natural form. But too much to give it up forever. And the thought of being tangled into others forever is . . ."

Another shudder.

"Grotesque," Hobbes offers. "Limiting."

I nod Jeanne's head and feel heat come to her cheeks.

Hobbes smiles and nods seriously, dragging on her cigarette.

"You're greedy," she laughs. "But I am, too. So I understand."

I smile. I knew she would.

"Still," Hobbes breathes. "They're not all the way wrong."

My attention piques. I hadn't expected that.

"Living symbiotically. As a collective," Hobbes hands me the cigarette. "That's something that we can't get around. It's not possible for us to live alone. It's too dangerous. By sharing resources and looking out for each other, we are safer. We can live longer. We can experience more."

I fight to keep the surprise off my face. I hadn't expected to hear that word from Hobbes. Symbiotically. I fight a frown at the mention of the word. The word I originally thought of as a key to unlocking my own freedom.

It's become a chain—a shackle.

Hobbes's eyes travel the length of my body as I consider what he said. I feel Jeanne's skin pimple and put the cigarette to my lips to hide my reddening. One inhale makes me cough immediately. Smoke pushes out of my body.

Hobbes laughs.

"We'll work on that," she says, taking the cigarette back. "Let's go find you a new body to test drive. Is there anything specific you're looking for?"

"A woman," I say without thinking. The woman from before flashes into my mind.

"Something stronger . . . more powerful."

Hobbes looks from Jeanne to her current body.

"Something even stronger if you have it," I push.

She smiles.

"I think I have something for you."

She motions for me to follow her. She steps out of her chair, walks towards the door, and pauses before going through.

"You know the rules of this place, right?" she asks. "If you want to use a body, you must provide one for the group."

Jeanne's skin pimples more.

I pause longer than I want to. I was supposed to be prepared for this.

"I know," I finally say. "Whoever wants this one can borrow it while I'm in another."

The familiar smells of candles, incense and perfume hit me as we enter the basement.

I'm suddenly nervous.

"But once I'm done, I'll be taking her back," I whisper to Hobbes.

She smiles.

"Sure. If you still feel that way once you're done, we'll talk."

XXXVII.

Her thigh and abdominal muscles ripple.

It's almost as satisfying watching and feeling them as it is to feel the body below me thrust deeper and deeper.

This body isn't as sensitive as Jeanne's. My insides feel duller. My skin feels thicker to the touch. It's still pleasurable, but I'm taking greater joy from the control and strength I have.

From where I am, astride another, I can see myself in the mirror.

Lithe but pronounced muscle amidst the tangle of bodies. I pull another body closer and feel their mouth on mine. Their hands play their way around the muscles in my shoulders and chest.

"You look like you're enjoying the new body," the other says with a smile before another kiss. They continue to toy with me until another pulls them beneath the tangle.

My eyes go back to the mirror.

I don't like her face.

She looks like so many of the faces down here—subdued, hollowed out, like some bit of life has been siphoned out of them alongside their conscious energy. Thankfully, I can hide it some with this body's mane of blond hair.

My eyes travel through the tangle of limbs and bodies. There are so many different shapes and variants.

Waves of pleasure start to give way to an awareness of the sheer amount of us crammed into this space.

We're all over each other. Intersecting each other.

My skin crawls.

With a small push of my larger muscles, I separate myself from the tangle. Surprise is evident on some of the nearby faces but they're quick to resume their fun without me.

A hand comes to rest on one of the bulgier muscles of my arm.

My bicep. I'm informed by a voice so drowned and far away I barely register it.

"Not exactly what you're feeling for right now?" the woman touching my arm says.

Hobbes?

No, it's the same dirty-blond woman. But she feels different.

"I figured when you chose that body, this might not be all you want to try," she says, leading me away from the tangle.

Her voice is softer now than the one Hobbes used. Her smile is decidedly less crooked as well.

XXXVIII.

"How does that feel?"

The woman who is not Hobbes holds my hips as I pull my legs above me.

Sweat drips down my brow. My arms burn. A smile pulls my lips back from my barred teeth.

"Incredible," I just barely breathe out.

"If I let go, do you think you can hold it?" she asks, already loosening her hold.

She doesn't wait for an answer. She lets go and I immediately feel more strain on my core. My shoulders and arms scream louder as I hold myself in place.

"There you go. Scorpion pose," she claps. "All on your own."

Sweat drips on the mat below me, but for several more seconds, I hold myself in the pose, exhilarated by the strength and flexibility of my body.

I hold for a couple more seconds before I finally fall on the mat.

"So, was I right?" she asks, holding out a water bottle.

Jasmine. She had said her name was Jasmine.

"You were right," I gasp, reaching for the bottle.

I don't know how much time has passed.

I turn over, panting, and stare around the small "gym" she had led me to. At the various machines, equipment and materials scattered around. Almost all of which Jasmine has explained to me in some detail.

We had started with "lifting weights," but had quickly moved over to the mats for what she called "Yoga."

It was thrilling.

It was not as pleasurable as the acts from the previous room, but it was full of more targeted sensations. Each exercise allowed the exploration of a different body part and muscle group.

"Why didn't Hobbes recommend this?" I ask Jasmine when I catch my breath.

She laughs, shaking her head a bit.

"Hobbes is more interested in the pleasures that a body provides than the fulfillment that can be gained by using one," she smiles.

I think of how many tries it had taken Jasmine and me to complete the scorpion pose, the strain of each movement, and the difficulty of learning to engage different muscles.

Fulfillment.

A positive feeling that comes from developing your own skills, my host defines.

Her skills.

I didn't develop them. I'm just using them.

I let my eyes wander down this host's muscles in the mirror. My hand follows, and I frown at the feeling of my host's taut, coarse skin.

"Can any body become this strong?" I ask.

"Most, with a little effort," Jasmine answers. "Although women tend to be more flexible than men. So for these poses specifically, it might take a bit longer as a man."

I smile hearing that.

"How often would you need to practice?"

Jasmine laughs.

"It's called 'working out.' And you'd need to do it at least twice a week for a few months to get into shape. And up to a year to get this pose. Of course, we cheated by using a body that was already strong and flexible."

I nod my agreement with that last part.

Twice a week for a few months.

Annoyance flickers through me as I think of the picture of Jeanne holding the skin on her side.

"Thank you," I say after a while, "for showing me all of this."

"It was the obvious thing to do," Jasmine shrugs. "You chose the strongest woman's body we have. I figured you'd want to make use of those muscles and that flexibility."

I look over her host's similar muscles.

"You said Hobbes doesn't like this, and he seems to favor the body you're currently in," I point out.

The now-familiar, easy laugh falls out of Jasmine.

"Oh no," Jasmine manages through laughs, "Hobbes doesn't prefer being this body. He prefers having this body."

I don't understand.

"Hobbes enjoys having sex with more sensitive women," Jasmine explains. "Playing with them. He finds them more entertaining."

Thoughts of Jeanne flash in my mind.

"Although you gotta be careful about using hosts after Hobbes," Jasmine warned. "He sometimes breaks them."

My heart thumps below the muscles of my chest. Fear begins to creep up from my stomach.

"I think I should go soon," I say, looking for the exit.

XXXIX.

We exit the gym and reenter the scented darkness of the main room.

It takes a minute for my eyes to adjust. A hole opens in my stomach before I even see. A hole opens in my stomach the moment I can.

"See, like I said. I wouldn't want to occupy her once he's done," Jasmine frowns, shaking her head.

In the center of a tangle of bodies I see Hobbes back in the body of the large dark man. Unmistakable by the crooked grin, he grips Jeanne by the neck.

Heat spreads through me.

The hole in my stomach becomes a chasm.

My muscles clench so hard my teeth grind.

Hobbes directs the other three around him, each toying with different parts of Jeanne's body. I can't take my eyes off them as they touch her.

A pained but lustful smile flickers across her sweaty face—an expression I've never seen on her before.

One I never want to see again.

Jeanne's skin wrinkles under someone's grip. Her body arches in response to the thorough movements of the others. Her hair is taut in Hobbes's hand.

I'm reminded of the shower I took nights before. The pain of catching my hand in a knot of Jeanne's hair.

The hole in my stomach is closed by the fire coursing through me. I take a step forward.

"Don't worry," Jasmine says, placing a hand on my arm. "They probably won't break her. Let them have their fun."

"They're being too rough," I hear come from me as a low growl.

Jasmine nods and strokes my arm softly.

"A little bit of pain can be fun," she says softly. Then, with a grin, she says, "Want me to show you?"

It takes no effort to break through her grip on my arm. I didn't even mean to do it.

I walk into the mass of bodies. Some stop as I pass through them. Others continue.

Hobbes sees me coming and turns his crooked grin around.

"Having fun?" he asks.

I pull him off of Jeanne.

Not quite as easy as breaking Jasmine's grip, but it's not difficult either. These muscles are useful.

"What are you doing?" Hobbes demands, breaking my grip on him and swatting my hand away.

Around us, everyone stops.

"You're being too rough," I explain, doing my best to keep the fire in my chest out of my voice. "Jeanne is sensitive."

Hobbes brushes himself off and rises to his feet.

"That's kind of the point," he says. "Don't worry, we're not going to cause any lasting harm. I wouldn't want to ruin a body such as this."

"You'll leave marks," I say. The growl in my voice returns. "She'll notice. She'll stop taking the pills."

Hobbes looks confused.

"I'm ready to leave now," I assert, placing myself between him and Jeanne who is now sitting, staring up at me. Whichever of us inhabits her now is clearly confused.

I separate a piece of consciousness and let it drift over to Jeanne. I open my boundary and feel it intersect the one currently inhabiting her. A much smaller entity.

GET OUT! I order.

I feel Jeanne's consciousness begin to leak as the other detaches and I let go of my current host.

My vision flashes in and out as I switch bodies.

It's a little disorienting.

I've never switched hosts this quickly. I find myself staring up at the muscly back of my former host and the no-longer smiling Hobbes.

My body's sensations flutter in. Pain. Less than expected. Weakness. Dull, lingering throbbing sensations. Some leftover pleasure.

"You're breaking the rules," Hobbes states in a flat voice.

The look on his face doesn't match his tone. Every muscle in his face is clenched and his forehead and undereye darken further.

"Let's calm down," Jasmine says softly with a hand on Hobbes's arm. She stares into me.

Scared. Imploring

"We've all gotten attached to a host, but you can't do this. You need to give that host back to Hobbes."

I stare past her at Hobbes. Barely hearing her over my anger.

"We lent you a host, the use of this space and everything in it," Hobbes growls. "In exchange, you lent us the use of your host. Until we're done, you can't have her back. Those are the rules here."

Some murmurs and nods around me. The muscly woman I had been inhabiting earlier, now the host to another, takes a few steps behind Hobbes and turns.

"I didn't get to finish either!" she says with a pout. "It's not fair!"

My heart begins to beat faster. I'm surrounded.

"I can't let you have her," I say, feeling smaller. More uncertain.

On unsteady legs, I rise and back towards the exit.

Hobbes says nothing. He watches me wander over to the door and attempt to turn the latch.

It's locked.

"I want to leave," I turn and tell him. My heart beats faster. I look for other exits.

Hobbes's face goes blank and I feel a much larger boundary intersect mine.

I would also like you to leave, he rumbles into my boundary, *but I'm keeping your host.*

She's mine, I shout before I can stop myself.

Desperate.

Realizing the full truth of it.

No other host feels like this—weakened as she is. Flawed as she may be.

Hobbes erupts.

She's yours because I let you have her.

His voice rips across my boundary. Memories of watching Jeanne walk through the park. Feelings of inhabiting her as tests. Frustration when I beat him to it. And then the decision to let me have her and take home the consolation prize 'host.' Knowing I would bring her to him at some point.

I close my boundary. He doesn't understand.

She is mine.

And I have to get her away from him.

I feel conscious energy begin to leave me and flow into Hobbes. It's like the first time I met the ones in the sky. I try to draw conscious energy back into me, but I can't match the flow. I'm losing far more energy than I'm bringing in.

How?

Years of practice, comes the answer. The question must have transcended through my boundary.

My boundary is shrinking too fast.

I could stop it by closing my boundary. But then I would lose my connection to Jeanne and leave her stranded here.

I can't.

I won't.

I do my best to increase the amount of conscious energy I'm drawing from Hobbes. I shut my boundary everywhere I can without losing my connection to Jeanne.

It's no good.

I can draw some, but not enough.

You learn quickly, but you're out of your depth, Hobbes says through both his boundary and out of his mouth.

Only a small amount of strain is visible on his face. He's too old. Too strong.

I try again to draw more energy and, this time, succeed. My rate of shrinking slows down.

Stupid, an irritated Hobbes spits in a "voice" that reverberates through me.

He completely encapsulates me; again, I feel how massive and old he is. He tears my boundary open where it was closed. How?

He draws a massive amount of conscious energy from me. I can't hold on. Energy drains from me rapidly and . . .

. . . nothing.

Silence.

Or rather, the lack of hearing.

I'm out.

In between.

Floating in my form, pins and needles twinging at the tip of my shrunken boundary.

What has he done?

I feel for every form around me. I look for the color of Jeanne's conscious energy and realize what's happened.

Hobbes hasn't done anything.

Jeanne's woken up.

XL.

She's awake.

No conscious energy is leaking. I can feel Jeanne's consciousness flicker as she frantically moves around. She's panicking.

I wish I could hear her.

What will she do now?

An image of the bowls of drugs and the unconscious bodies being laid out flashes into my mind.

What will they do to subdue her?

I need a host.

But even with a host, I would just be trapped inside with her.

I need a plan.

I fly around the building looking for any available host, for any person who can be useful. There's no one, no one who is uninhabited.

I fly through the walls and open my boundary. I'm so small. There won't be much margin for error.

I spread myself out as far as I can, waiting to intersect.

I can feel the closed boundary of the doorman. But there has to be an opening. And if Hobbes can do it, so can I.

There!

I begin to pull as much conscious energy as I can. He isn't prepared. I'm able to draw significant amounts of conscious energy before he even tries to pull any back. I ignore the panic and questions coming through his boundary.

There's no time.

His boundary closes as he escapes my onslaught. And conscious energy begins to leak from the host body.

I dive in.

I can hear muffled screaming through the door.

Jeanne's voice.

I unlock the door and wrench it open. She's staring right at me, eyes wide. Several people try to hold her back. Behind, I can see two people running in with needles.

Sedatives, my host informs me.

I reach out and pull her forward.

Simultaneously, I push the others back and try to pull the door closed. The doorman's bulk makes this easier than it would have been in another body. But I still can't close it completely, with the others clamoring to get it open.

I feel several boundaries intersect mine. They begin to draw energy. A muddled chorus of angry thoughts and voices all at once.

I'm suddenly thankful for Hobbes and the elders above. Because of the practice I've had with them, I'm not only able to protect myself but also draw energy from them.

My reserves replenish and some of the smaller, weaker ones fall away.

Hobbes may be old and skilled, but so many of these ones are not.

"Get away from here," I yell at the terrified and confused Jeanne.

She doesn't move. She just looks from me to her body, then up the stairs. Her eyes are wide.

Why isn't she moving?

I finally realize.

You stupid humans and your concern around nudity.

I rip the robe off of one of the people trying to get past me and throw it backward as I hold the door.

"Go!" I yell.

She mumbles a weak "thank you" as she puts on the robe and disappears up the stairs.

I let myself relax for a second and Hobbes's enormous boundary begins to pull at mine. The others recede as they get caught in his attack.

Don't let her go, Hobbes orders through my boundary through controlled rage. *If she goes, she'll be out of both our reach.*

I know he's right. She'll stop taking the pills after this. The fear in her eyes told me that much.

But still.

I have to hold here for long enough for Jeanne to get away.

I do my best to draw energy back from him. He increases the intensity of his power draw.

He was playing with me before.

He could have killed me easily.

He might this time.

Because of the practice, I'm barely able to withstand for a minute before I'm forced to close my boundary.

Relief.

With my boundary closed, both the energy being siphoned out of me and the chorus of angry voices halt.

I fly up the stairs and through the walls, stopping only to observe the various colors of conscious energy at the street level.

I can't feel Jeanne.

She's escaped.

She's safe.

My somewhat replenished boundary flutters with relief.

That was very foolish.

The massive form intersects me and Hobbes's angry voice reverberates through me. He must have left his host. His whole form is stifling in its vastness. I can't even feel his nucleus, just the massive void of his expanse.

It's so heavy, I can't move.

Segments of my boundary tear open again. I try to close it but instead I feel the rest of it rip open. Conscious energy steals from my body quicker than I've ever felt.

My boundary screams.

Please! I manage to communicate through my entire form. Desperate.

I gave you a chance to leave her and go, he communicates. *I gave you a chance to let us get her back. No one takes from me. You get no more chances.*

Cold. Dismissive.

He rips at the last of my conscious energy. I can't do anything against it. I start to feel the pins and needles alongside the pain from the assault. There's not much left of me.

I focus all my energy on closing my boundary, giving up on drawing energy from him.

I manage to close most of my boundary, but one segment straggles. I need to close it.

If only for a second.

Just one second.

There!

Relief floods through me as the assault stops. Pins and needles prickle my nucleus. And I try to think of a way out.

Not enough.

Hobbes's voice grumbles as my boundary is wrenched open

again.

He could have done this at any point. I stand no chance.

Pain screams through me.

I feel the full brunt of his feelings now.

He doesn't care about Jeanne. He's furious that a high-quality host was taken from him. But he won't go after her.

I'm in tatters. I'm torn and shredded. I give up.

The last of my energy flows out of me.

What's left of my boundary brushes against my nucleus. Pain explodes through my form. For the first time, my core shudders.

I can hear it now.

That same scream I've heard so many times before. The scream of one of my kind fading out of existence.

Only this time, it's coming from me.

My core begins to shatter.

I think one more time about Jeanne.

About all the things I had learned.

Meeting the ones above.

Meeting Hobbes.

I open my boundary.

With a final push, I try to share one final thought with Hobbes: a memory and two words—two words I had learned when we met.

At the same time, I pull as hard as I can.

Desperate. Determined. Formidable.

Wait!

XLI.

I ignore the drunk dizziness of my current host.

I run a hand along my arm. I let my eyes wander around me. The lights from various clubs hang in the air, and crowds of people filter into cars. The lights are pleasant. The heat of other humans warms this one's skin.

I explore the entire experience of this human.

Good. But not enough.

I separate and float through the storm of conscious energies.

Something nips at my conscious energy. I bite back as Hobbes had taught me. A quick opening of my boundary and the hardest pull I can manage without killing it.

Sharks, Hobbes had called them. Though they're not so different than how I used to be.

Starving. Desperate.

This one scampers away to find easier prey.

They fill this area, making it a difficult hunting ground for our kind. The younger and less capable risk death here.

Not me. I am up to the challenge. I've lived through worse.

I inhabit another human.

A girl strokes my arm as I sit in a car. My limbs are powerful and smooth. I'm larger than her. My vision is blurred. The sick feeling in my stomach is strong. Blood rushes below my waist.

Not this one, either.

I separate.

Another tries and regrets nipping at me.

"They're not like us," I remember Hobbes explaining. "They're instinctive and predatory. They have no interest in taking hosts. They survive only off of the energy of their own kind."

"Not many can handle them," he had smiled as I recharged. "But you should be able to."

Another host.

This one shivers in the cold. He's dressed warmly, but he still feels cold. A man's hand rests against the small of his back. His heart beats in quick bursts. I run my hand through his hair and down his neck. His skin tingles.

This one.

I shake off the other man's arm and walk away. He's confused. He says something I don't hear.

His words are lost in the wind as I walk away.

XLII.

Early morning sun breaks through the clouds.

Shadows of buildings invade the familiar park. The sunlight hits my host and lessens its shivering.

It's a welcome change.

Hours of sitting in the early morning cold haven't been pleasant.

The building door at the end of the park opens and I rise from the bench I'm sitting on. I feel the mass of conscious energy behind me move as well.

The woman approaching is small and soft. Her clothing is accented by bright colors. Her eyes are ringed in red.

She's preoccupied. She doesn't notice me approaching her on the empty path.

I bump her shoulder softly as I pass.

"Oh, sorry, I wasn't paying attention," she says in her soft voice.

"No," I say. "I'm sorry, Jeanne."

Her eyes go wide as she hears her name. Wider when I grab her arm. Fear and tears flood them when the hand in my pocket pulls out a syringe.

"Why?" she manages as I push the plunger.

I search for an answer she'll understand. I can't come up with one. There's not enough time to remind her of her neglected travel board. Her obsessive work. To tell her that she's not making much use of her body.

To explain that I'll take better care of it.

I cover her mouth and wait.

It doesn't take long.

Her body slackens and I can feel her consciousness wane. I leap out of my current host and into her.

I breathe deeply as I'm reunited with this body.

My body.

Both the man beside me and I stand up.

"Not a bad consolation prize," Hobbes grins, running his arms along the body I had picked out. "I think I'm going to enjoy this one."

"I'm glad it meets your approval."

I don't really care as long as it fulfills our arrangement.

I reach out a hand.

He pulls a collection of pills and syringes from his pocket. Things I had picked up from his house earlier.

"You still owe me two," he reminds me as he hands everything over. "That was the deal. Two to replace the one you stole. And then another one to supply you with all of this."

I nod.

A mutually beneficial arrangement. In a way my relationship with Jeanne could never be. For now and moving forward.

Symbiotic.

"I'll deliver another to you as soon as Jeanne goes to sleep," I promise.

"Aren't you Jeanne now?" Hobbes asks. The trademark crooked grin surfaces on the young man's face.

"When I'm in this body," I say, thinking of the picture board in her apartment. The travels I plan to schedule. The food I plan to eat. The human experiences I plan to explore.

"And when you're not?" he asks.

I feel my boundary dance around me. My expanse diminutive in comparison to Hobbes. I imagine flying through empty skies, feeling the warmth of new and unexplored climates.

The enjoyment of being in between.

"Then I'm who I've always been."

Hobbes smiles. Understanding.

"You've found another path," he concedes. "One host isn't enough for me, but I'm interested in how this goes for you. It may be something I offer future members."

XLIII.

I was wrong about Jeanne.

Or, more specifically, our relationship. We weren't symbiotic. Not in the way I wanted.

We were more like the ones above. Flying tethered to each other.

I stare at the photos scattered across the table in front of me. Torn down from their ceremonial place on the picture board.

She was never going to go on these trips.

She wasn't going to lose the weight.

She couldn't even keep her apartment clean.

And she would eventually become as limiting to me as those tangled masses in the sky are to each other.

My taste buds dance as the first slice of pizza passes my lips. I sink into the couch and, with my free hand, massage the bruise forming on my legs from where I had pinned myself down earlier.

I want to make this body stronger. That's the first thing I'll do.

After that?

I would need to rebook the vacation. Search for travel options. Jeanne's faint voice tells me what I'd need to look for. Hotels. Flights.

Who knew humans could fly as well?

I can't wait to experience it.

You're greedy, I hear Hobbes laugh.

He was right. This whole time.

Not all the way. But more right than wrong.

I want it all. I want to live in all the moments. Not just those in between.

Free of pain. Full of life.

Experiencing everything.

In both my forms.

I search my consciousness for Jeanne and barely feel her.

So far below the surface.

Consciousness. Body. Life.

Surrendered to me.

I reach for another slice of pizza.

Teneō

latin. verb.

- To hold, have.
- To possess, occupy.
- To watch over, guard, defend.
- **To restrain, control, keep.**
- **To imprison.**

Kojo Gyan is a Black Canadian writer and sometimes comic based in Vancouver, BC. Channeling an urbanite upbringing and love for fantasy, his writing brings daydreams to life by building chimeric renditions of our everyday world.

Read more at **kojogyan.ca**

Made in United States
Troutdale, OR
04/22/2025

30844229R00094